For Better or For Worse

Book 1 in the

"Til Death Us Do Part Series"

Krissy V

FOR BETTER OR FOR WORSE
Copyright 2014 Krissy V

Dedication

I have always lived by the rule that "Everything happens for a reason!"

My life changed when I received my kindle as a gift for my birthday in 2011, through this medium I met a lot of indie authors who really did change my life.

This book is dedicated to them. Thank you for showing me that if you have a story to tell, there will always be someone who will want to read it.

It is also dedicated to my family who have supported me through writing this whole series, who have accepted me and my laptop as being "one".

I love you all and hope that I make you proud!

Playlist

From This Moment – Shania Twain
Russian Roulette – Rihanna
I Need You Now – Olly Murs
Grenade – Ariana Grande
Skyscraper – Demi Lovato
Been A Long Day – Rosi Golan
Just Give Me A Reason – Pink
Numb – Linkin Park
Read All About It – Emeli Sande

IT'S MY WEDDING DAY and I'm so excited to be getting married to the man I love. The man I would move to any corner of the world to be with. The man I want to have children with.

When I first met this man he swept me off my feet, he showed me a world I could only dream of. He treated me like a queen and gave me gifts. He looked after me like a girl wants to be looked after.

This man is Felix and Felix is all mine!

I walk down the aisle on my Dad's arm, I look at him and see tears in his eyes, when we pass my Mum she's crying too! I look towards the altar and see Felix smiling at me, I smile back, I think about how lucky I am to be marrying this beautiful man, he's beautiful inside and out. While I'm walking closer to the altar I smile thinking about how we got engaged, it only seems like yesterday, although it was 6 months ago. We had gone out for a few drinks with our friends and later in the evening we said our goodbyes and went home, we got a taxi because we had both had a few drinks. When we slid into the back seats of the taxi, Felix pulled me tight into him and started kissing me and forcing his tongue inside. I took it gladly and offered mine back to him, which he took. His hands were starting to explore my body and I felt so turned on, all of a sudden the taxi stopped and the driver cleared his throat "We're here you might be more comfortable inside" he chuckled.

I laughed but Felix doesn't like it "how much?" he asked gruffly and then went on to pay the driver. Felix is very protective of me and treats me like a lady, he likes to make sure that I am treated like a lady, he doesn't like anyone swearing in front of me, he says it's disrespectful. He's quite old fashioned in his ways. He makes me feel like a princess all the time and he can't do enough for me. Only the day before our engagement he had brought me breakfast in bed, a tray with a cup of tea and a single red rose. He sat on the edge of the bed while I had my breakfast and chatted to me, we never seem to run out of things to talk to each other about.

After we went into the house he closed the door behind him and gently pushed me up against the wall and devoured my mouth, he was as horny as hell and I could feel how horny he was through his trousers. He pulled back and took my hand and pulled me up the stairs, when we went into the bedroom he said "Don't turn the lights on Tasha, I want this to be romantic" he slowly took my clothes off, then he gently pushed me onto the bed and then told me to move up the bed. When I reached the pillows he told me to stop and I did! He was very commanding, but I loved it! He climbed over the top of me and then he took my two hands and raised them above my head and said "Keep them there Tasha. Don't move!" I didn't dare move, I didn't want to.

He kissed every inch of my body, making sure he concentrated on the place between my legs. He licked me and sucked on my lips and pushed his finger inside me, I bucked my body up and then pushed down so that I could take all of his finger inside. He took his finger out and then plunged two fingers inside me, this made me groan. "Felix, please!" I shouted "I need you, all of you, please"

He moaned against my lips and this nearly made me lose control, all I wanted to do was to reach down and push his head down so that he couldn't move, but I didn't, he asked me not to move my arms, so I didn't. He pulled his fingers out and crawled up my body, when he reached my mouth he stuck his tongue into it and kissed me deeply. When he pulled away he said "Taste yourself Tasha, you taste delicious" he put his two fingers into my mouth and I tasted them and licked them. It tasted good!

He took his fingers out of my mouth and ran them down towards my breasts, I couldn't cope any longer. "Felix please" I begged. He reached across the bed and took a condom from the drawer and slowly pulled it on. He smiled at me and then he leaned above me and slowly started to push himself inside me. The feeling of him entering me is like no other feeling, it makes me feel complete, makes me feel whole! He pushed in and out "Harder Felix, harder" he did what I asked.

Then he said "You can move your hands now". I didn't wait any longer and moved my hands down, it hurt a little from keeping them in the same position for a while, but the pleasure I had in grabbing his ass far outweighed the pain. I pulled his ass closer to my body and with it pulled him deeper. I couldn't hold on anymore and I felt myself going over the edge. "Felix oh my god" this turned him on even more and he was slowly following me. "Tasha I'm cuming" I felt his cock getting bigger and then he spurted his hot cum. He lowered himself down on top of me, sweating "I love you so much Tasha, I really do" he kissed me on the side of my face as he lay on top of me.

After a few minutes he pulled out of me and went to the bathroom to take his condom off. When he came back he walked over to my side of the bed completely naked and then all of a sudden he went down on one knee "Felix, what are you doing? Get into bed and give me some hugs" I said because it looked like he was looking for something, I slowly sat up and looked at him, he had left the bathroom door open slightly so that I could see him clearly.

"Tasha I love you and can't imagine a day in my life without you. I want to grow old with you; have children with you; I want to have you by my side every day of my life. I never want to be without you in my life. You are so important to me. Natasha, will you marry me?" He looked at me pleading me with his eyes.

Everything went in slow motion, I looked at Felix naked and down on one knee. I looked at the bed and only then realised it was covered in rose petals, he must have done this before we went out. Oh My God! Felix had just asked me to marry him! I looked at him and I reached out and took his hand "Yes, Yes, Yes" I almost shouted at him because I was so excited. He smiled and leaned forward and kissed me "Thank you, you have made me the happiest person in the world Tasha. You won't regret it, I love you"

He took my left hand and slid something cold onto my finger, wow was all I could think. It's beautiful! The ring was white platinum with a large diamond at the top standing proud, then on the ring going from the top to half way down each side there were smaller diamonds encrusted into the platinum. "Wow, just wow Felix! This is beautiful, I can't believe you did all of this for me" I could feel the tears in my eyes, I was so happy!

"Yes I did Tasha, you deserve this and so much more, when I saw the ring I knew it would suit you so much, it's elegant and beautiful just like you" he stood up and walked over to his bedside locker and took out a bottle of champagne and two glasses, he really did think of everything. He climbed into bed and poured two drinks and handed one flute to me. "Here's to me and you Tasha and our perfect life together"

I shake my head to bring me back to today, my perfect day!

When I get to the altar, Dad passes me to Felix, who takes my hand and smiles at me, he leans across and kisses me on the cheek "You look so beautiful today Tasha" I smile back at him and the registrar carries out the ceremony.

We agreed on having a civil ceremony because Felix said that we weren't church goers so it wasn't right to have a church wedding. I always wanted a big white church wedding, but I suppose he was right. This room where we are today is beautiful, the chairs are all covered in white cloth and have a bow tying them onto the chair, the ribbon is peach colour to keep it understated. The big picture window in the room is overlooking the gorge and of course my favourite view in all of Bristol, The Clifton Suspension Bridge.

The wedding ceremony goes without a hitch and as we had decided on having our wedding here at the Avon George Hotel, we went out onto the terrace to have our wedding photos taken with the Bridge in the background. I always go to The White Lion Bar in the Avon George Hotel when I need to think, the view just makes me feel peaceful and thoughtful. I was delighted when Felix suggested this hotel because it's beautiful, central for everyone coming for the day and the views are amazing.

When we have finished taking all of our pictures for our wedding album it's time for the meal. Everyone sits in their places as per the table plans and then me and Felix walk into the room as man and wife. There is a lot of cat calling and whistles as we walk past the tables and up to the top table, where Felix pulls the chair back and lets me sit before pushing my chair back in. I look at him and I smile, he is so wonderful and I am so lucky!!

The meal is gorgeous; everyone seems to be enjoying it. We've had our dessert and the speeches are just starting. This should be fun. Felix's best man, Luca stands up and I can hear everyone whispering, they are obviously going to have a bet on how long the speeches last! I wonder who will win.

He says "Ladies and Gentleman can you all raise your glasses in a toast to the bride and groom" everyone stands and says "The bride and groom." I blush because everyone is looking at me. I don't really like to be the centre of attention.

He then does his speech, which is funny, laugh out

loud in places and long. Next to get up is Felix, he does the usual "On behalf of my wife and I" and everyone starts clapping, again they are all looking at us and I blush. He says thank you to the right people and everyone seems really happy. Next he looks at me and asks me to say a few words, WHAT?? This wasn't agreed, what does he want me to say?

"Felix, I haven't prepared anything, I don't have anything to say. What do you want me to say?"

He leans down and says in my ear "Natasha, just stand up and say something, they are all looking at you to say something, don't embarrass me now by not standing up when I have introduced you"

I'm really annoyed with him, but I stand up and say "Hi everyone, I don't have anything prepared but I just want to say thank you to everyone for coming to this our very special day. I'm so lucky to have married this amazing man, he is gorgeous on the inside and on the outside. Now, I want you all to go to the bar, have a drink and come back ready to party!" There are lots of cheers and whistles, our friends like to party!

Everyone walks out to the bar and me and Felix split up to make sure we talk to everyone. I'm really annoyed with Felix, I didn't like the way he spoke to me, he's never spoken to me like that before.

"Hey baby" I hear in my ear as Felix comes sliding up behind me. "Sorry about earlier I just thought it would be nice for you to say something too. You did well babe!" He kisses me on the cheek.

"Thanks I just don't like being put on the spot, but I did do ok didn't I?" I say turning around and leaning up to kiss him on the lips. "Isn't everything just so perfect?"

I say with my arms wrapped around his neck.

"It's always perfect when you're involved babe" he says and leans down and kisses me passionately pushing his tongue in past my lips. I hear a moan and realise it's me.

"Come on let's meet some more guests and then we can party!!" He says

We split up again and go around chatting to everyone. We are asked to go up for our first dance and we get on the floor to "From This Moment" by Shania Twain, the words to the song just spoke to us when we were planning the wedding, it's beautiful and romantic, I'm so happy to be Mrs Parrish.

About midnight Felix whispers in my ear "Are you ready to seal the deal?" I laugh and nod my head. Felix goes over to the band and asks for the microphone. "Ladies and gentlemen, thank you for coming along to celebrate our marriage, Natasha and I wish you all the best but we are leaving early in the morning so we will be leaving now" Felix says with a big smile. Again there are catcalls and whistles.

We go up to the honeymoon suite in the lift and I can't keep my hands off Felix, he looks so gorgeous in his suit, he is so handsome, how was I so lucky?

We reach our suite and he lifts me up across his body and carries me into the room and lays me gently on the bed. He then says "Stand up babe, you look so gorgeous today I could just eat you, actually wait you're my wife I can eat you anytime I want to" he has a big grin on his face.

I stand at the bottom of the bed while he undoes the small buttons on the back of my dress, halfway down he gets impatient and just rips the rest of the buttons and they fly across the room. I turn around and glare at him "What the hell Felix? The dress is too nice to do that to" I'm really mad at him.

"What's the fuss for Tasha? You're not going to wear it again" he says ripping the rest of the dress off me.

"That's not the point" I say looking him in the eye "It's my wedding dress Felix, it's special!"

"Come on Tasha let's get you out of it, I want to take what's mine" he says staring into my eyes with that gorgeous smile he has. I never could resist that smile.

I smile back at him and say "Come and get it then hubby"

I don't need to say anything else, he comes up to me and removes all my clothes and underwear in one swift move, I don't know how he does it, but right now I don't care!

THE MORNING AFTER THE wedding we have booked an early alarm call because we have to be on a flight at 8am, luckily the hotel isn't far from the airport and we can eat breakfast there.

When we arrive at the airport, we find the check in line and stand in the queue. Felix holds my hand and periodically leans down and kisses me "I'm so happy we're married Tasha I can't believe it" he smiles. Anyone looking at us would realise we were newly weds because we can't stop touching each other or kissing. When we've checked our bags in we go through security and then to the restaurant to have breakfast, we have two hours to kill before we board the plane.

We talk about yesterday and how well it all went, who was there, what everyone was doing. I'm exhausted and can't wait to sleep on the plane, the flight is just over 13 hours. We have to take a 45 minute flight to Heathrow and then we fly to Dubai where we have a few hours before the flight to the Seychelles. It's a lot of travelling, but it will be worth it to spend some quality time with Felix: no wedding to organize; no work to discuss; just the two of us together, 24 hours a day for the two weeks. My idea of heaven!

When we land in the Seychelles there is a town car waiting to collect us, Felix booked the Honeymoon, I didn't have any idea where we were going until the day before the Wedding, he told me "We are going to The Seychelles - pack accordingly." I don't think I had a clear idea of what I wanted for a Honeymoon, but Felix knew from the moment he asked me to marry him where he wanted to take me, so it was easier to just let him organize it. It was busy enough organizing the dress and flowers as it was.

When we arrive at the Four Seasons Hotel, I am in awe! It is so beautiful here, the hotel overlooks the Indian Ocean and also a rainforest. We go into reception to check in and the Bell Boy brings our bags in and takes them to our room. Our room – wow! We must have the best view of the whole island, I can see for miles out on the balcony. The Indian Ocean is almost turquoise in colour and it's surrounded by lush green rainforest. The two colours complement each other so well it's like they belong together, just like me and Felix.

When we have finished looking around our room – it's called the Serenity Villa and I can see why, we make good use of the emperor sized bed and the start to our Honeymoon. There are many bars and restaurants in the hotel so we don't need to go outside our resort, it's a very relaxed atmosphere and we just take it easy. There is a spa and I make sure I take the time to take some treatments.

The two weeks we spend here are wonderful, just the two of us and Felix has been so happy, and that makes me happy too. Although one night we had quite a few drinks and there was a couple at the bar, we had seen them there a few nights, but they were always arguing, I noticed because they were very loud. Anyway, this particular night, the guy was on his own and he had drunk a lot, he started leering at me and trying to chat me up. Felix was not amused and started to get in the guy's face, I had to pull him away and take him back to the room. He was going mad, shouting and I caught him trying to smash one of the vases in the room.

"Felix, stop! You're scaring me! The guy was drunk and he'd obviously fallen out with his girlfriend" I grab his arm and try to pull him down onto the couch. "Felix" I say when I get him on the couch, I then climb onto his lap and straddle him so that he is sitting in place and I can grab both sides of his face in my hands so that he has to look at me and then I kiss him. This helps to calm him down and he kisses me back roughly, then he puts his arms around me and pulls me close to him. "Sorry Tasha" he says when he calms down "That guy was really annoying me, he was close to touching you and I didn't like that" he pulls me in even tighter. We made love again that night but it didn't feel the same as usual, it felt more emotional, rushed and slightly rough.

The rest of the Honeymoon went without a hitch and we had a fabulous time. He is so attentive and can't do enough for me, I realise that I'm so lucky to have him in my life.

We talk about children and wonder whether I am pregnant already. That would be fantastic, but I don't think I am, I don't feel like I am.

We start planning our life now that we are married. I know that when I go home and back to reality I have to start looking for a new job because the one I have involves travelling around the country and I know that I don't want to be away from Felix for too long anymore. I talk to him about this and he feels the same, he hates when I have to travel and stay overnight without him. I do, however, feel he is a little hesitant in me working somewhere else, I can't quite put my finger on it, but I think I'm more excited about the prospect than he is.

Soon enough we are on our way back home and, again, we stop in Dubai, but we stay the night this time. It is an amazing place and I can't believe what a fabulous time we have both had over the last two weeks, the best way to start our married life together. We lived together before we were married so it's not new to us, we've always had our own friends and had time apart to do things with our friends, even though we did live together. I'm sure that will continue, there's no reason why that should change and anyway we don't want to crowd each other. Working together and living together can be difficult sometimes, we are just lucky that we don't argue or fight so we don't take any bad moods into work.

3

WE WERE HOME FOR a few days when we had to go back to work, life is good! I started looking for a job as soon as I got home, I'm an Administration Manager and look after paperwork and facilities. It's a "catch all" kind of a job. It's because we have three sites situated around the country that I have to travel and I don't want to anymore, I want to be at home with my husband of an evening not sitting in a hotel room on my own. I find a couple of jobs I'm interested in and apply for them. I'm excited because I've been in my job for 5 years and I love the work that I do, so it will be nerve wracking to start somewhere new but it will be challenging too.

I hear back from two jobs and I've arranged interviews with them. One is for a Marketing Company, Blue Eye, doing an Administration Manager's role and the other is for a Facilities Company, Clifton Asssociates, looking after their premises, it's similar to what I do now, but they only have offices in the Bristol area where I live.

I'm very lucky that both interviews are arranged for early mornings so I don't have to have time off work, this makes it a lot easier for me.

The first interview goes very well and I really like Helen, the HR Manager for Blue Eye, I like their approach to work, they are relaxed but you can see they work hard. There is a second interview stage with the Operations Director and then if that is successful there is a meeting with their CEO. Wow, that's a lot of interviews, but they are a prestigious company and want the right fit. I finish the interview, shake Helen's hand and tell her that I look forward to hearing from them.

I leave the company with a smile on my face I really want this job. I ring Felix to tell him the interview went well but he's not as enthusiastic about it as I am. I don't understand why. I thought he would be happy that it went well. I go to work and don't get time to think about it because today I have some new procedures to implement in each department and I know I will see Felix shortly, he works in the Sales Department.

I remember the day that I first met Felix, he started working at my company and, as I look after the Facilities Management, he was introduced to me on his first day. I had to help him with his office and his requirements for his computers and his furniture. When I saw him that first day, I couldn't breathe, he was so beautiful standing there in the middle of an empty office and he just stared at me and at that moment I hoped he felt the same about me.

He is dark haired, with a style that is longer on top and shorter at the back and sides. He has blue eyes that are like a pool you can dive into. He had a small bit of stubble, like a five o'clock shadow even though it was only 10 in the morning. He was dressed like he had just finished filming an advertisement for Armani. Wow he was stunning, a very handsome and striking man.

We chatted for a couple of hours and as well as organising his office we had arranged our first date. Felix was the catch of the office, he was funny, he always knew what to say to cheer me up and he could always make me smile. The other girls in the office were always jealous of me when I started dating Felix, they would always make jokes about trying to steal him away, but luckily, Felix only had eyes for me.

It's a bit strange working with him but we don't normally bump into each other during the day.

When I go down to his department, he comes to meet me and says "I'm not happy about you looking for a job somewhere else Tasha" he seems angry "I won't be able to keep an e...I won't be able to help you with jobs. I enjoy that babe!"

"I know you do, but I'm not stretched enough, I need more of a challenge. Anyway it won't be good for our marriage to work together, share the same work colleagues and live together." I smile at him, but I heard what he was going to say, why would he want to keep an eye on me? He is starting to act really strange and I can't quite put my finger on it.

"I'd rather you didn't mention it in the office darling, I don't want anyone to know I'm looking for another job just yet" I say rubbing his arm.

He grumbles something then walks off with a backward glance he says "We'll talk about it later Tasha" and he stomps off.

Wow, what is going on with him, he was never like this before we got married, it's like he's changing in front of my eyes. I do the presentation to his department showing the new procedures we will be implementing and all the time I can feel Felix staring at me. I don't like the feeling at all. I shrug it off and go back to my department. The rest of the day passes quick enough and then I'm on my way home, when I get in I start preparing dinner so that when Felix comes home his dinner is ready, he likes his dinner to be ready, he doesn't like to wait.

We sit down to dinner and there is a silence between us, I decide to say something "Felix are you ok? You're very quiet tonight"

He stops eating, puts his knife and fork down and looks me in the eye and says "You looked like a tart today when you were giving the presentation, all the lads were staring, your top was too low!" he sneers at me.

"What? I don't believe you just said that to me, that is so hurtful" I start sobbing, I can't believe he talked to me that way, he never has done before.

"I can't believe you went to an interview dressed like that, of course they will give you the job dressed like that, they probably think they can look down your top everyday" he looks so angry.

"It was a lady that interviewed me" I say during sobs "there is nothing wrong with my top and what gives you the right to say that to me anyway?" Obviously that was the wrong thing to say, he gets up from his chair and strides over to my side of the table and grabs my ponytail and pulls it so hard that I have to look up at him "YOU are my wife and no one else will look at you with lust in their eyes, only I'm allowed to do that" he lets go of my hair, walks back to his chair, sits down and resumes eating his dinner. I'm sitting there with my mouth open staring at him with tears running down my face. I don't know what to say, so I just sit there.

He looks at me then says "Go and wipe your face you look a mess."

I get up from the table and go out of the room to the downstairs toilet and sob silently. What the hell just happened out there? I clean my face and then go and sit back at the table, I'm not hungry now so I just sit there with my head bowed down. I don't want to look at him!

"So babe, tell me about the interview, how did it go?" he says still eating his dinner. Is he serious?" Come on tell me!" he's starting to shout!

So I tell him about Blue Eye and Helen, the HR Manager and about the three stages of interviews, I tell him I'm really excited about this job and that I loved the company. He sits there nodding his head at me and asking a few questions.

"I have another interview with Clifton Associates, a Facilities Company tomorrow, the job looks good but I think today's job would be better all round" I say waiting for him to say something.

"Sounds good, let's see what happens, good luck tomorrow" he says. He stands up, puts his plate in the sink and says "I'm going to watch TV" and walks out the room.

He's being so weird, normally the two of us would do the dishes and chat about the day and what's ahead for the week. I try to ignore it and just do the dishes and then I walk into the lounge. "Don't forget it's Luca's birthday this weekend, we are going to Jesters for a party on Saturday night" I say, I'm really looking forward to going out.

"I don't think we'll be going" he says and I look at him with my mouth open "What?!" I shout "He's your best friend Felix, you have to go"

"I know who he is Tasha, I don't think it's our scene anymore, we don't need to go out and party every weekend" he says still watching the TV and not looking at me at all.

"It's not every weekend! It's this weekend and this is not a night you can back out of" I'm astounded that he wants to back out, he likes his drink as much as the rest of the lads.

"I DON'T want to go! I want to stay in" he shouts "don't you listen to me". He's getting really angry now, I don't understand it at all. He never shouts and especially not at me. Obviously he had a bad day. "Ok if that's what you want. I'm tired and I'm going to bed" I say and go up the stairs. I don't even know whether he said goodnight or not. I get undressed and put my nightdress on and slip under the covers. My mind is racing, what could be wrong with him, he is acting so weird, I can't believe he doesn't want to go out for Luca's birthday, Felix always wants to go out when Luca is going out. I fall asleep but know I'm in for a restless night.

4

I'M HAVING A DREAM about Felix and he is being really romantic, he's bought me flowers to apologise for his behaviour. I smile, then he looks at me with lust in his eyes and starts touching my breasts through my nightdress, this dream feels so real. He lifts my nightdress and then he takes one of my nipples in his mouth, he's flicking it with his tongue. I moan and then his other hand moves down between my legs and he starts rubbing my clit. I'm really enjoying this dream. All of a sudden he bites down on my nipple and I scream, it hurts, I sit up in the bed, my heart racing and Felix is sat there with no clothes on, smirking.

It was obviously not a dream and he was touching me while I was sleeping. "Felix Oh My God! What were you doing? Why did you bite me?" I ask because I'm so confused.

"I wanted you to wake up, I didn't want to have to masturbate, I wanted you to do it for me, you are my WIFE after all" he says looking up and down my body.

"Felix, what is going on? You're not yourself at all today" I ask wrapping my arms around myself. I feel like he is looking at me like a piece of meat or a piece of ass.

"Nothing's wrong with me babe I just want you, I want my wife" he says licking his lips, he looks like a hungry fox. He starts to push me back down on the bed. I struggle a little bit because I'm really not in the mood, he treated me badly earlier and now he wants to have sex with me.

Who does he think he is. "Felix get off me, I was asleep, leave me alone. You've been horrible to me all night and now you want to have sex with me. No! It's not happening"

He looks so angry as he pins my hands above my head and laughs "You think that just because you say no - it means I'm not going to take what belongs to me. You really don't know me if that's the case" he's ripping my nightdress with his free hand and scratching me at the same time.

"Felix please stop" I'm sobbing now and shouting "please stop!"

"I'm not going to stop until I'M ready to stop" he says as he's ripping my panties. He seems to be enjoying me struggling against him, so I decide that it will be easier not to struggle, so I just go limp and let him do what he wants to do. He finally cums and pulls out. "Now that was the best sex we've ever had" he says as he gets off me and walks into the bathroom. I get up and go out to the other bathroom and lock the door. I run the bath and when it's ready I get in it and sob. I can't believe what he just did to me, and I can't believe the way he is treating me at the moment. I lay in the bath for about an hour, I don't know what I'm going to do, who can I talk to? No one will believe me, I don't know if I can believe what just happened myself, how could I convince someone else? I lift the plug out and let the water drain out around me, it feels like I'm being pulled down through the plug hole, like all my worries draining away, but I know that's just not true.I dry myself off and go into the bedroom, Felix is fast asleep sprawled out on the bed. I want to go into the spare room and sleep, but I don't know how he would react to that and I don't want to annoy him just in case he does something else to me.

So, I slip into bed beside him and roll onto my side as far away as I can get. I eventually fall asleep.

I made sure I set my alarm extra early because I didn't want to be in bed when he wakes up and I needed to get ready for my next interview. I get out of bed and go into the bathroom to have a shower and put my make up on. When I walk back into the bedroom, Felix is awake, he looks at me and says "I've put your clothes out that I want you to wear to the interview, I don't want you looking sexy for anyone else only me" I don't know what to say, I'm speechless. On one hand I want to tell him where to go and that he can't dictate what I wear or do and on the other hand I don't want a repeat of last night. Ever!

I look at him and say "I'll wear what you want me to wear if it makes you happy" I have to look away because he smiles like he has won a prize.

"Oh baby that makes me so happy" he gets up off the bed where he was sitting and walks over to me. He reaches out to give me a hug and I flinch, he looks angry but he still wraps his arms around me and hugs me tight.

"I love you babe" he kisses me, I try not to kiss him back but he just gets more aggressive in his kiss, so eventually I have to kiss him back, even though it makes me feel sick "See how much easier things are Tasha when you do what I want" he says, he let's me go and then walks off to the bathroom.

I put on the clothes he left for me:- a dark trouser suit and a high neck blouse!

I let a breath out that I didn't even know I was holding, I can feel my shoulders slump and I can feel a tear falling down my cheek. I rub it away and turn to go downstairs "I'm going downstairs to put the coffee machine on" I say to the bathroom door, I don't know whether he heard me or not because I just walk out of the room.

I go into the kitchen and put the coffee machine on and start preparing our breakfast, I usually have muesli and Felix has toast. I can hear him coming down the stairs so I put an empty bowl in the dishwasher pretending I have eaten, because right now I don't think I can eat without vomiting everywhere. Felix sits down and starts eating his toast "I'm going off to my interview now" I say busying myself with my handbag "I'll see you at work later"

I turn to walk towards the front door and he catches my arm, I stand still, he pulls me to him "Don't I get a goodbye kiss? I Love you Tasha" and he kisses me. I let him, then I walk towards the door. "Oh and Tasha I'll take you to lunch today"

I just say "OK" and walk through the door and into my car.

5

WHILE I'M DRIVING TO my interview I get time to think. How has my perfect life changed so drastically in 24 hours? And why me? What has happened to my husband, Felix, and what am I going to do about it? I know I can't go to Mum and talk to her, she thinks Felix is flawless, he is like a walking God in her eyes. Kammie isn't much different, she's seen how good he has been to me and how he makes me happy. I realise there is no one for me to talk to, hopefully it won't happen again and I don't need to talk to anyone about it.

I push all those thoughts out of my mind and concentrate on preparing for my interview; this would be a good move for me too, not as good as Blue Eye, but good all the same.

When I arrive at the building I walk in to reception and announce myself. The receptionist is gorgeous and very smiley, she asks me to take a seat and the HR Manager will be with me shortly. I sit on the sofa and watch the coming and goings of the staff. Everyone seems happy, it certainly looks like a good environment to work in, I start to feel positive again. This is what I need, a change, a challenge!

I'm asked to follow the receptionist down the corridor and into a room where I'm asked to wait for a couple of minutes and the HR Manager, Debbie will be joining me. I take those couple of minutes to look around at the surroundings, it all looks very nice. Just then the door opens and Debbie comes in and introduces herself, she's a lovely bubbly person and I like her instantly. The interview goes well and again there are a couple of interview stages, after Debbie there is an interview with the Operations Manager and he has the final say. I say thank you to Debbie and leave, I'm confused now because I like both jobs, they have both got great potential.

I stroll back to my car, it's so warm I'm starting to sweat in this shirt, I'm thinking of taking my jacket off it's that warm. As I get near my car my phone rings and it's Felix "How did the interview go babe?"

He sounds happy "Hi, it went well, I really liked the company, I hope I get another interview"

"I'm sure you will babe you're very good at your job" he says "What time's your lunch I want to take you out somewhere nice"

What is going on, I can't deal with this yo-yo behaviour. "I can go anytime that suits you" I know I don't sound enthusiastic but I can't pretend nothing out of the ordinary happened last night.

"Great I'll pop into your office around 12.30 babe. See you then" he says and hangs up the phone not giving me an opportunity to say anything.

I think again about ringing Kammie, she's been my friends since kindergarten, she should be able to tell me what to do, but I just don't think she'd believe me, no one would, Felix is such a nice guy, even I don't understand what's going on. I arrive at work and have to put my thoughts of chatting to Kammie behind me, I need to concentrate on my work.

The morning passes really quick as I have a lot of projects going on at the moment, I have to go to our office in Plymouth for 2 days next week, so I need to catch up on everything before I go. Soon enough, there's a knock at my door and the door opens "Hey babe" Felix says coming up behind me and sliding his arms around my waist and kissing me on the neck. "Are you ready for lunch? We are going to Piccolino's."

I stand up "Yeah I'm ready let's go" and I follow him out to his car.

It's quiet in the car on the way to Piccolino's and then Felix surprises me "Sorry about last night babe, I was in a bad mood and I'd heard some of the lads at work talking about how sexy you were when you bent over the table to talk to one of them, I just don't like the thought of someone looking at you like that. You're MY wife!" I can see his hands are tightly wrapped around the steering wheel and his knuckles are white.

"I know you were in a bad mood Felix but you didn't need to take it out on me, I didn't do anything wrong".

"I know" he says and I can hear remorse in his voice "I'm sorry, let's have lunch and enjoy it, then after work we can go shopping and buy you a new sexy dress for Lucas's birthday party" he smiles. I sit there staring at him, was it just my imagination that he was a bit rough on me last night? Was I blowing it out of proportion? Now I'm just confused.

He parks the car, he takes my hand and we go into the restaurant, we have a lovely lunch and then we go back to work. Felix was very attentive over lunch, he knows that Piccolino's is my favourite restaurant, it wasn't a coincidence that he chose to take me there. As we go to my office, he turns and says "See you later babe, I'll be back to go shopping at about 6pm" he kisses me on the forehead and walks away, leaving me not being able to say anything, yet again. I shake myself and get on with my work, at least I know what I'm doing when I'm at work because I don't really understand what is happening in my home life.

Felix comes home at 6pm, he is always punctual. We go to the shopping centre and he follows me around while I look for a nice dress to wear for the party. I go into Donna Karan and find the perfect dress, Felix loves it too. I turn and say to him "Do you like it? I absolutely love it" he looks me up and down.

"I won't be ale to keep my hands off you on Saturday night, I will be so proud of my wife" he says.

I can feel tears welling in my eyes, this is the Felix I love, this is the Felix I miss. "Thanks darling I thought we weren't going to go and I'm so glad you changed your mind."

"Yeah I'm looking forward to it too" he says. I change back into my work clothes and when I've come out of the changing room, Felix has paid for my dress.

"Thanks darling I can't wait to wear it Saturday night now" I say linking arms with him. We have 3 days to go and I'm so excited, I must make sure I ring Kammie and see if she is coming out Saturday, I miss her when I haven't seen her for a few days. I've known Kammie since Kindergarten, we have been best friends from the first day when we both ran into the room and tried to sit on the same seat. We banged into each other and then both fell on the floor, when we looked at each other we started laughing and I don't think we've stopped laughing since. I love her like she is my sister and up until now I've told her everything in my life, I ask her opinion on everything and I don't keep secrets from her. I feel sad that I don't feel like I can talk to her about this, I just don't know how she would react. Would she believe me? Would she laugh at me and think I wanted some attention now the wedding is over? I don't think she would, but I don't want to risk losing our friendship over something she might not believe and something that I don't understand.

When we get home I take my dress upstairs and hang it up in the wardrobe, I do what every woman does when they get a new dress – I found all the accessories to match:- shoes, necklace, earrings etc, then I smile to myself and go back down to the lounge where Felix is waiting for me. We cuddle up together on the couch and watch TV, then when we go to bed, Felix pulls me in to his front and puts his arms around me and holds me tight. Before I fall asleep I smile and think that maybe I was just imagining it and he wasn't really rough with me last night, maybe he was just showing me how much he loved me.

The next couple of days fly by and it's Thursday lunchtime when me and Felix are out to lunch in the local brasserie and my phone rings, I don't recognise the number but answer it anyway "Hello Natasha speaking" it's Debbie from Clifton Associates.

"Hi Natasha, hope you are well, I really enjoyed our chat on Tuesday and wanted to invite you to an interview with the Operations Director, Mr Wolfe, on Monday morning. He can see you early to accommodate your present job" This is great news!

"Wow that would be great thanks. So 8am with Mr Wolfe, I'm looking forward to it. Thanks Debbie and have a nice weekend" I say hanging up.

Felix is looking at me strangely. "Who was that?" he asks.

"That was the Debbie from Clifton Associates, she was inviting me back for a second interview with Mr Wolfe, the Operations Director" I say smiling. Felix smiles "That's great news, that company is really good I know someone who works there" Oh right this is news to me, he didn't mention it when I talked about this job before. Strange!!Then again, everything seems strange right now.

The afternoon is really busy and I've just about caught up with all my work when it's time to go home. I drive home, smiling to myself because I am excited about the interview. My phone starts ringing and I answer the phone "Hello Natasha speaking."

"Hi Natasha, this is Helen from Blue Eye, we want to invite you to a second interview which will be with the Operations Director" she says "Oh wow that's great news" I say "Yeah we are looking at Tuesday morning at 8.00am if you can make it" she asks "That's great, I'm travelling to Plymouth later that day so that's perfect!" I say smiling really widely." Perfect, the interview will be with me and Mr Wade, the Operations Director" she says.

"See you Tuesday" I say happily.

I can't wait to tell Felix, I am so excited. I start cooking dinner when I walk in so that when Felix walks in his dinner is on the table. He walks in and comes over to me and puts his arms around me and pulls me to him and he kisses me forcefully, but not in a bad way, in a way that turns me on." Something smells nice and I'm not talking about the dinner" he says close to my ear, he pulls my hair back off my face and kisses me on my neck, I can hear myself moan, it feels so good.

"Felix dinner is nearly ready, stop" I laugh. He moves behind me still kissing my neck and I can feel his erection brushing up against my buttocks, it feels good. "What do you want first Felix? Dinner or dessert" I say smiling.

"Hmm" he says "I think dinner smells nice but I bet dessert tastes nicer" he's still kissing my neck "Hmm I think I might take dessert first tonight, put the dinner on hold and then turn around and kiss me properly" I don't wait for him to tell me twice, I turn the hob off and turn around to face Felix, he looks so handsome tonight, I want him so badly. He leans forward and kisses me and I kiss him back, he forces his tongue into my mouth and I suck it and then I take his bottom lip in between my teeth, he loves when I do that.

He starts to take my dress off, he unzips the back of it and it slides onto the floor, he steps back and appraises my body "Jesus Tasha, you are smoking hot tonight" he moves forward again and I start undoing his shirt and I pull it off him. He lifts me up onto the work surface kissing me all the time, then he rips my panties off and I think back to the other night, but I push it to the back of my mind, this feels so different. He pushes me back slightly and starts touching my breasts, he then kisses each of my nipples and starts kissing and licking down my stomach until he gets to my belly button, which I have pierced, and he takes my bar into this mouth because he knows that it drives me insane when he does that. I moan really loud and I stretch and lean back thrusting my pussy closer to his face. He doesn't disappoint me and he kisses down from my belly button to the top of my shaved pussy and he puts his tongue in and licks my clit, I groan even louder.

"I think I need some cream on my dessert" he says "don't move an inch" he walks over to the fridge, opens the door and pulls out the squirty cream. He turns around and smiles at me as he walks over to me in a predatory fashion. "Now don't scream when it comes out it will be freezing cold" he says licking his lips. I wait with anticipation of the cold and he doesn't disappoint me, I hold my breath when he starts squirting the cream onto my pussy and when he has finished he licks every drop off and I have an unbelievable orgasm. He stands upright and while I'm coming down from my orgasm he drops his boxers and pushes his cock straight into my pussy.

"Wow Felix, that feels amazing" I can see that he is enjoying it too.

"Tasha this feels so fantastic, you are so sexy babe, I love you so much" he gets faster and then he slows down and pulls his cock almost all the way out and he squirts cream on it, then he uses it as lubricant, not that he needs it, I'm so wet already. He only manages to pump his cock in another couple of times and then he cums and I quickly follow him. He leans over me and pulls me into a hug and kisses my head "I'm extra hungry for my dinner now" he pulls out of me and then pulls me off the counter and slaps my ass "Now make my dinner, wife of mine" he laughs. We both get dressed and I have to go without panties as he ripped them, again!

6

BEFORE I KNOW IT it's Saturday and me and Felix go out for lunch after a lazy morning in bed. Everything is perfect again and we are both happy and looking forward to the party tonight. After lunch we take a stroll around Cribbs Causeway, not really looking for anything, it's just a nice way to kill a couple of hours. Then we drive home to get ready to see our friends, obviously it takes me longer than Felix to get ready, but it's worth it to see his face when I'm all dressed up. He looks like he could eat me. "Wow Tasha you look gorgeous" he says as he looks me over from head to toe "Take your panties off, I want to think of you wearing nothing and being ready for me anytime I want" he says as he walks towards me in a predatory fashion.

I gulp as he stops in front of me, he reaches out and lifts my dress and slowly takes my panties down until they're on the floor and I have to step out of them. He drops my dress back down and then he picks my panties up and sniffs them "Mm I can't wait to taste you later, it will turn me on knowing I can take you anytime and you will be ready for me" he says as he stands and reaches around my neck and brings me closer to him so he can devour me with an earth shattering kiss. He pulls away and says "Are you ready babe? Let's go and have some fun" he puts his arm out for me to link and we leave the house. We get into the taxi that is waiting outside and go to Jesters, where Luca has reserved a private party area at the back of the club. I'm looking around for Kammie, she had text me to let me know she was coming tonight and I can't wait to see her. All of a sudden I am knocked sideways and it's Kammie "Hey Tasha, how are you bitch I haven't see you for ages" she's gushing and pulls me into a bear hug, Felix just laughs and walks off to find Luca. "So tell me, how is married life? Bet you're at it like rabbits" she laughs. "Yeah we are" I say not quite looking her in the eye, I don't want her to ask me something that I have to lie about. "Let's meet up in the week and we can have a good talk, tonight is for partying" I say, hoping she doesn't catch on that something is wrong.

"Yeah good plan, now lets get this party started bitch" she says dragging me off to the others "Hey guys the bitches have arrived. Let's party!" she says waving her arms in the air. She always likes to make a scene and she is so confident, she loves being the centre of attention, unlike me, I'd rather just drift into the background, Kammie never lets me though. We both go to the bar and get a drink and I feel a hand slide around my waist and I smell Felix so I lean into him "Hey babe did you get a drink yet?" he says into my ear. His hand slowly lowers down to my hip and I can feel myself getting warm and a bit wet between the legs. "Yeah I just got one now. There's a good gang tonight, I just know it's going to be lots of fun" I say turning around to kiss him. Kammie says "Oh god come on guys. Felix put her down" she's laughing when she says it though, she doesn't mean it. He moves away from me and then he walks off to find Luca.

"So Kammie, any news?" I ask "No, not really I've been busy at work you know the usual" she says shaking her head.

"Nothing happening on the guy front?" I ask her, I know she likes Luca and I'd put money on it she wants to go home with him tonight. "No. Nothing exciting anyway, I met this guy last week, he seemed nice but he's been stalking me all week. I told him it was a one night thing but he didn't believe me. I think I'll stay away from men tonight, although seeing as its Lucas's birthday I might have to give him a present" she laughs.

"Kammie what are you like?" I'm laughing too "Come on let's dance" she says dragging me off to the dance floor. I see Felix looking my way so I indicate that we are going for a dance, he nods his head and turns back to talk to Luca.

Me and Kammie like to dance, we can lose hours on the dance floor and we can forget about anybody except ourselves when we are dancing. It's getting pretty crowded and we've had a few drinks so we like to spread out when we are dancing, you know - arms and legs everywhere, but there isn't enough room to move. I indicate to Kammie that I want a drink and we move off the dance floor and go to the bar. There's no point going to the bar in the private area because this one is closer to the dance floor and we've not danced enough yet.

We get two bottles of beer each because it saves us going to the bar again for a while. Then we get a shot of tequila with the salt and lemon to go with it. We do the slammers and then drink most of the first bottle of beer as a chaser. We burst out laughing when we've done that and I can feel myself getting unsteady. I don't really like the taste of Tequila, but it's a kind of ritual that we do when we are out, so I just knock it back. We go back to the dance floor carrying our beers, hoping to find a table to put them on while we dance.

We get to the edge of the dance floor when someone pushes me to get past me and I stumble into a man and spill my drink on him, he just about catches me before I fall to the ground. "Whoa steady, where are you going?" he pulls me upright and I say "Oh my god, I'm so sorry I tripped and I can't believe I spilt my drink on you. God I feel terrible. Let me wipe it up"

I start to wipe his jacket with my hand, he takes my hand and says "It's fine don't worry I know it was an accident" he has a real deep husky voice that vibrates through me, it makes my girly bits start to throb, I must have had more to drink than I thought. I finally look up into his face, wow is all I can think and then I realise I said it out loud, the man and Kammie are looking at me." Did I just say that out loud? How embarrassing" I say laughing, but really I'm embarrassed.

"Wow is right, my god you are beautiful" he says holding me upright "and you're drunk. Are you sure you didn't hurt your ankle or anything when you stumbled?" he asks with sincerity in his voice.

I can feel his hand on my bare arm, there is so much

heat coming off his hand, but it's the buzzing feeling travelling up my arm and into the rest of my body that is making me feel strange. I've never felt this kind of electrical shock before, I must be really drunk. I try to shake my head to clear it slightly. "No I'm fine, I just dented my pride" I laugh. I look into his eyes and they are so beautiful, they look deep and the colour is a beautiful shade of green, amazing! I just keep staring into them. "Can I? Erm, can I pay for your dry cleaning bill? I'm really sorry I don't make a habit of throwing my drinks over men" I laugh, I am so embarrassed, but I am also tingling all over.

"No it's fine, honestly it was going to get cleaned anyway" he smiles at me, then I see a reaction of some kind in his eyes so I look away from them and then I find his lips, but then I can't stop looking at them, they look so luscious, so soft. I realise I am staring at him when he says "Actually, maybe you can" I drag my eyes away from his lips and look him in the eyes, I look at him a bit confused, I obviously haven't been listening to him. "I will take your number and then I can arrange for you to get my suit cleaned." I've heard of someone having a "twinkle" in their eye, but I've never seen it before, until now. He definitely has a twinkle in his eyes. I'm so drunk at this stage and still reeling from his touch on my arm that I say "Oh yeah sorry, of course I'll give you my number, sorry I don't know what's got into me" I give him my number and tell him to let me know how much it is and that I will reimburse him. Me and Kammie go back to the dance floor, but I can still feel his eyes on me and my skin is tingling from his touch.

After about 15 minutes we realise it's so busy that

we can't even dance. We are on our way back to the private party when Luca comes looking for us "Hey Kammie I was hoping for a birthday dance, come with me please?" She doesn't need to be asked twice.

"Luca" I say before he walks off "Where's Felix?"

"I think he's outside he wasn't very happy, he looked really angry, so I think he went for some air. I don't know what made him like that, you know Felix he's usually so placid. It was strange" and with that Kammie drags him on to the dance floor.

I wonder what's got into Felix and I walk outside to find him. I see him leaning over the wall, I wonder if he's drunk. I walk up to him and slide my arms around his waist." Hey Felix, what are you doing outside?" He turns around and just stares at me.

"What the hell was going on downstairs on the dance floor? I came to find you to see if you wanted to dance and I saw you in the arms of a stranger" He has now moved so that I am stood with my back against the wall and his arms are on either side of me blocking me in.

"Felix, I tripped and spilled my drink all over that man, I don't even know who he is, honestly I've never seen him before" I move my arms to put them around his neck to kiss him, to show him that I only want him.

He pushes my arms away, "Don't touch me right now Tasha, I'm too angry. Just don't!" he stands back a little, then he grabs my wrist and starts dragging me behind him "We're going home, we need to have a chat" I try to protest but there isn't any point as he just keeps pulling me.

He drags me along the side of the dance floor where

I had fallen and he drags me right past the stranger, who stares at me and mouths "Are you ok? Do you need help?" I just shake my head and look at the floor, I am so embarrassed. I can see Luca and Kammie, they look like they are getting on really well, I'm happy for them. They look over and see Felix, and see him dragging me behind him, Kammie says something to Luca and he walks over to us.

"Felix, what's going on? Where are you going? And why are you dragging Tasha behind you like that?" He puts his hand out to stop Felix, who had absolutely no intention of stopping.

"Luca, mate, please move out of my way. Me and Tasha need to go home and have a chat, she needs to remember who she is married to and how she shouldn't be talking to strangers and giving them her phone number" Felix almost spits out the words, he is trying to get past Luca, but Luca is stronger than Felix.

"Come on mate, you don't need to talk to Tasha about that, she knows that and she would never to do anything to make you think differently, what is really going on here?" I can see Luca is getting annoyed with Felix, the one thing that Luca cannot stand is a man using his power to intimidate a woman.

"Luca, just get out of my way or you might regret it. We've been friends for years and I intend for us to remain friends, but right now you need to let me go and take Tasha home." Felix is trying to get past Luca all the time he is talking.

"No Felix, you have to calm down right now, I am not letting you leave here in that mood and take Tasha home, I have never seen you like this, what has got into you?" Then he turns to face me "Tasha are you ok? What is going on?"

I start to sob a little, "Luca just let him past, please?" I can feel myself pleading "Felix isn't happy because when he came to find me on the dance floor he saw me talking to a stranger who I had spilt my drink on when I tripped. Now he thinks I was up to something and I wasn't I swear"

"Felix, this isn't you mate, come on calm down, please" Luca takes his hand off Felix and Felix takes the opportunity to drag me off again.

Felix stops and turns back to look at Luca "Luca, this doesn't have anything to do with you mate, please just leave it! I've calmed down but I just want to go home now it's been a long day. I'll ring you tomorrow ok? Maybe we can all do lunch or something" Felix is gripping my wrist really tightly, so I say "Yeah Luca let's do lunch tomorrow, our treat, Kammie you come too, it will be nice" I smile at them.

Kammie hasn't said anything the whole time Felix and Luca were arguing, she is just staring at me, I know she is trying to work out what is going on and what she can do to make the situation better. I just shake my head at her, I can feel tears pooling in my eyes and I know she just wants to hug me.

Luca obviously decides that he can do no more and steps out of the way. Felix says "Thanks Luca, me and my wife need some alone time" and starts walking away.

Luca and Kammie look at me being pulled behind Felix and ask am I ok. I just nod my head, because what else am I supposed to do. Luca makes a hand gesture that says ring me if you need anything. I nod and turn back to concentrate on Felix. I see Luca take Kammie's hand and pull her into him and then he says something to her, she looks at me and gives me a half smile. They turn and walk back to the VIP room.

When we get outside Jesters there is a cab waiting, luckily. Felix drags me into the cab and then sits as far away as he possibly can." Don't touch me right now Tasha, I'm so angry" I just sit looking out the window on my side of the cab. I have silent tears running down my face and I can see my reflection in the window, it's not a pretty look. I try to wipe them off, but they just keep falling. I've never seen Felix like this and I don't like what is happening to him.

When we get to the house, Felix doesn't say a word, he pays for the cab and then goes into the house. I reluctantly follow him, not knowing what will happen when I get inside.

As soon as the door closes, Felix locks it and then he drags me upstairs to the bedroom." Do you want me to treat you like a slut? Because that's what you looked like tonight when you were hanging all over that guy" his face is bright red and he looks like he is going to explode. He is shouting at me, his face only inches from mine.

I try to protest but it doesn't make any difference "Felix, I wasn't all over him, if you had arrived a minute earlier you might have stopped me falling rather than him. I swear Felix, you know I love you more than anything in this world, come on, please" I try to reach out to touch him but he pushes my arm away.

He comes up to me, making me walk backwards, until I reach the wall, then he just stands there looking me up and down "You love me do you? How much do you love me? Tell me Tasha, tell me!" he shouts.

"Felix I love you to the moon and back you know that! Why are you being insecure? It's not like you. You got to take me home tonight, no one else, you'll be taking me home every night, no one else" I try to think of something that might calm him down." Felix I want you, I love you" I start crying now, because I'm really scared. I hate how he can make me feel scared of him, because he never did before we were married, how did he keep this side of himself hidden until now? I just don't know!

"No! You're just saying that to try and make me happy, you don't really mean it, I saw you tonight, I saw you give him your number – why did you do that?" he asks as he closes the gap between us, he takes his hands and places them around my neck "Why Tasha, Why?"

I can't move, he has his hands around my neck, I can't get my words out very well, all I can feel is his hands getting tighter. "I said I would pay to get his suit cleaned, I was being nice, I ruined his suit Felix when I tripped and spilt my drink on him, I don't even know his name Felix, honestly" I'm crying when I'm saying all of this.

He slowly moves his hands away from my neck and he pulls me to him, he wraps his arms around me and hugs me so tightly I have trouble breathing." I love you so much Tasha, I just can't have someone coming in and taking you away from me"

"No one is going to take me away from you Felix, I love you" I hug him back, I'm so frightened right now, I don't want to make him any angrier.

Felix steps away from me and sits on the bed with

his head in his hands he looks at me "I'm sorry Tasha I don't know what's come over me, I know you love me, I just don't want you to leave me" I can see tears in his eyes. Where has all this come from?

I walk over to him and take his head and pull it to my stomach "Felix, please! I love you, you have to know that" I step back to look into his face, he is shaking his head and not looking at me.

I can feel my hangover starting to kick in because I have sobered up very quickly after what has happened between us since we got home. "Felix, I have to go and get a glass of water, I'll be back in a minute ok" I turn to walk out the door and this sets him off again, it's like flicking a switch.

"No! Tasha you are not leaving me, you said you wouldn't" he stands up and follows me out of the bedroom door, "Tasha, where are you going?"

"Felix I told you. I'm going for a drink. Calm down!" well that seemed to be the wrong thing to say, I can hear him catching up with me, but I need a drink. I have to get a drink and a couple of headache tablets because I can really feel this headache kicking in.I get to the top of the stairs and start to make my way down. Then I say "Felix, I have a headache and I need to take some tablets".

"You're going to ring him when you're downstairs aren't you? I know you are. Don't lie to me Tasha, don't lie" he is like a mad man, and when I'm halfway down the stairs he says "No one else is going to have you Tasha, just me, always me" and he pushes me down the rest of the stairs. I can't even tell you what goes through my head during the next minute, but I fall against the wall and bang my head, then I slip down some stairs and then land on my back, everything seems to happen in slow motion. I can just about see Felix's face as I bang my head on the floor and then everything goes black.

7

I CAN HEAR A noise.

It sounds like crying, continuous crying.

I can feel a pain, a really big pain in my head, in my ribs, in my heart.

Then I hear my name over and over again.

It's Felix!

He's telling me he loves me, he needs me and that I'm not to leave him, I promised I wouldn't leave him.

I just keep thinking that I'm not ready to leave, I'm not ready to die.

8

THE PAIN IS REALLY BAD, I can't talk, I can't tell Felix how much it hurts. Everything keeps going black.

I can hear Felix on the phone to someone and he's crying "Please come she fell down the stairs and she needs help" I don't know what they said to him but he says "No, I'm not calling an ambulance, she'll be ok, just come round and tell me what to do." He listens for a while then he says" They'll think that I did something when all she did was fall, please come now."

Everything goes quiet again and I drift off for a longer time this time.

When I drift back I can hear voices, two male and one female voice, I would recognise that voice anywhere, its Kammie. She is kneeling above me crying "Tasha, please speak to me, come on I don't know what's happened here and to be honest I don't care. But what I do need is for you to be ok, come on Tasha, please."

I hear Luca next, he sounds angry "Felix you need to ring the ambulance, she has been unconscious for too long, you need to get her help. I know she just fell down the stairs, but if you don't ring them, I will."

Felix doesn't say anything. Is he going to let me die?

"Felix. She. Will. Die. if you don't get her help" he is shouting at him and he pauses after each word, like he is trying to snap him out of whatever is happening to him.

"Ok, Ok can you ring them? I just can't do it, I'm scared Luca" Felix is crying uncontrollably.

I drift off again and then I hear the ambulance arrive and the paramedics lift me onto a trolley and take me into the back of the ambulance. I can hear Felix sobbing, "I'm sorry Tasha, I love you so much, come back to me"

I'm trying Felix, really I am, but I can't talk, I can't move, I'm so tired.

Then it goes black again.

I get to the hospital and I can feel myself starting to come around, the whole of my body hurts and I'm so thirsty. I open my eyes and look around me, Felix is holding my hand with his head bowed down. The doctor assigned to me, smiles at me "Hello Mrs Parrish, that's quite a knock on the head you got yourself" I try to smile at him, but I just hurt too much. I can feel Felix tighten his grip on my hand. "Tasha, oh my god, you're going to be ok" he kisses my hand.

I hear the doctor saying to Felix " Mr Parrish, can I ask you to step out of the room while we examine your wife and find out the extent of her injuries" Felix starts to protest, but the doctor ushers him out of the room.

I hear the doctor close the door and them he comes over to me " Mrs Parrish, Natasha, how are you feeling?

I'm going to examine you, you've had a bad bang to the head".

The doctor continues to examine me, it seems I have concussion and I have broken a couple of ribs, which will take time to heal, but that is about the extent of my injuries. They want to put a bandage around my rib cage and keep me overnight to check on my head wound. He starts to ask me how it happened and what do I remember?

I tell him that I was walking down the stairs for a glass of water, as I had a headache because I had drunk too much earlier in the evening. I was halfway down the stairs when I tripped and fell. I must have still been drunk. I remember Felix running down the stairs and calling the ambulance.

I don't know why I just lied, but it felt like the right thing to do, what goes on behind locked doors and all that!

The doctor finishes examining me and then walks to the door to let Felix in." Your wife explained how she tripped down the stairs when she was going to get a glass of water. She has a couple of broken ribs and a bad concussion, so we will be keeping her overnight to monitor her. Hopefully, she will be able to go home tomorrow"

Felix smiles "Thank you doctor, thank you, I was so worried about her and I'm delighted that she's going to be ok, thank you" he shakes the doctors hand and then he comes over to me and takes my hand and kisses it." Tasha, I'm so sorry" he whispers in my ear "I love you so much babe, you need to get better" he says louder for the doctor to hear.

After about an hour, the doctor asks Felix to leave so that I can have some rest. He stands and kisses me on the forehead and he says "I'll be back early in the morning Tasha, I love you" and then he's gone.

The doctor says that he will give me something to help me sleep and I'm grateful for it because I don't want to think about what happened tonight, I don't understand it and I don't want to. I lie there crying and can't believe I am in this situation. How did I get to be a victim? I have never been a victim. I'm strong and I never give up, but I know that by protecting Felix, I had become a victim. Maybe, just maybe, now that this has happened he might leave me alone.

I drift off to sleep and have an amazing dream about how my life was so perfect before I got married.

Mornings start early in hospitals and the nurse woke me at 7am to ask if I wanted breakfast. I said I would love some toast and a cup of tea, she said she would get some for me. She disappeared for a few minutes and then came back to check my vital statistics. She said that I was doing well and that the doctor would be in in about an hour or so and he would give me a once over and then probably send me home with some good painkillers. This piece of news both excites me and makes me nervous.

How are things going to be at home? What is going on with Felix? How am I going to be able to be near him? I don't know any of the answers and it really scares me.

Felix turns up at 9am and comes into me, "Tasha, how are you feeling today babe, you look much better than you did last night" he comes over and kisses me on the forehead. I try not to flinch but I must have because he says "Come on babe it was an accident, don't be afraid, I just want you to come home to me Tasha, I love you, I hate being apart from you"

"I love you too Felix" I say, but I'm not sure I mean it at this moment! I don't know what I feel!

"Luca and Kammie are coming over this evening for dinner, I said I would cook, they both want to know that you are ok. I called them last night when you fell down the stairs, I just didn't know what to do, I froze. They were here in the hospital last night too, but they weren't allowed to see you" he says all of this while rubbing my hand with his.

I don't know what to think, on one hand I'm happy that there will be other people in the house with us and on the other hand, I can't lie to Kammie, I never have been able to.

"Let's just see what the doctor has to say, I might just need rest with the broken ribs, hopefully he lets me home today" I say, not really meaning it.

I'm so confused, I don't know what I feel about what happened last night. I haven't had time to process it and I don't know that even if I had the time, would I be able to! This is all so new to me, I've heard of women who are scared of their husbands, but I never expected that to be me!

The doctor comes in around 10am and starts checking all my vitals and then he has a feel around my ribs and the strapping that is helping me to breathe without hurting myself. The pain is quite unbearable so he gives me some more pain relief." I'm not sure you're ready to go home Natasha, there is a lot of discomfort from your ribs, you will have to be on complete bed rest for a few days and even then you will have to be on pain medication" he looks from me to Felix "do you have someone at home to look after you Natasha?"

"Of course she does, she has me doctor" Felix says looking at the doctor.

"I know that Mr Parrish, but what about when you go to work? Is there someone who can keep an eye on her, help her to get dressed and do other daily tasks?" he looks at me with sympathy in his eyes "Are you ok with going home today Natasha?"

"Yes I'll be fine doctor, Felix will be able to help me and when he is at work, I have friends and family who will be able to help me out, please let me go home today and start getting better" I look at him and I know I am pleading, but I really need to get out of here and start processing what has happened.

"Ok then, if you're sure. I still want to keep an eye on you for another two hours or so and then you can go. Mr Parrish, why don't you go home and get all the arrangements made for looking after your wife for this week and then you can come back and collect her about 1pm, is that ok?"

Felix is reluctant to leave, but he knows he has to go and make some phone calls to get some help looking after me this week.

"Ok doctor's orders Tasha, I'll be back later to collect you babe" he leans forward and kisses me on the forehead. I smile at him weakly "OK Felix, you can get everything for dinner as well and then we can see Luca and Kammie this evening". All I want to do is go to bed when I get home. I don't know why he thinks I want to have friends over, even if it is Luca and Kammie. I just want to go to bed and think about what happened, about why I am in this hospital room and what I am going to do about it.

Felix leaves the room and I can feel the doctor looking at me "Was there anything else doctor?" I ask and I am surprised at my own hostility.

He looks at me some more and then sits on the side of the bed "Natasha, you were in a bit of a state when you came in last night and I noticed there was some bruising on your neck, how did that happen?" he's talking to me like I'm a child.

"I don't know, I must have hit my neck when I fell down the stairs" I can't look at him, I find it so hard to lie. I totally forgot about Felix putting his hands around my neck, it all starts to come back to me. It was better when I didn't remember.

"Ok Natasha, how did you fall down the stairs?" why is he asking me these questions? I already told him, I just don't understand it.

"I was going downstairs to get a glass of water because my hangover had kicked in and I missed a step because it was dark and then the next thing I know I'm here. I could hear voices around me, but I couldn't open my eyes. It was very scary" I said and I could feel tears in my eyes.

"It's ok Natasha. Of course it was very scary, I understand that, but are you sure you tripped?" he really is pushing me too far.

"Doctor, I told you I missed a step that's all, I don't like what you are insinuating. Please stop!!" I shout, I need him to back off because he is getting too close to the truth and I'm not ready to tell anyone yet!

"Ok, you missed the step, I get it. I'm going to let you rest before you go back home, I will be back in to see you and sign the discharge papers, I will also give you my number in case you ever need it. I will give you another number for you to keep in your purse, you never know when you might need it" he smiles at me and then pats my hand before he stands and walks out the door.

When he closes the door I can breathe again. Was he trying to insinuate that Felix pushed me down the stairs, he didn't, I tripped didn't I? I'm getting so confused, I don't think I know what really happened, maybe I just slipped, I was drunk after all.

A few minutes later I hear the door open and Kammie comes flying through the door and almost launches herself at me. I can see she has been crying." Tasha, oh my god I was so scared, you looked dead when I saw you at the bottom of the stairs, it was horrible" she hugs me as tightly as she can without hurting me "What's the verdict? When are you coming home?"

"It's ok Kammie, I have a couple of broken ribs and I banged my head, I had a concussion. So beside a big headache and a lot of bruising I'm fine, honest" I can't look her in the eye either.

"Tasha what happened? How did you fall?" I know she thinks she knows what happened, I can tell by her tone of voice, I can tell because I know her so well and she knows me too. She will know if I lie to her, but I don't know if I can say the truth out loud, and do I really know myself what happened?

"I missed a step Kammie because I was so drunk, me and Felix had an argument and I went stomping down the stairs in the dark." She takes my hand, making me look at her.

"OK, will we try this again? Or I can give you my version of events and you can just nod if you like" she knows I can't vocalise what happened." I think Felix was really angry for some reason, you had a fight, I believe you were heading down the stairs, but I believe Felix was right behind you and he pushed you, how am I doing so far?" god she really does know me "It might have just been an accident and I hope to god it was Tasha!"

I sit there and just nod my head, I hear her gasp, maybe she didn't really believe it was true. "Oh Tasha what are you going to do? The man I saw at the club last night was not the Felix we all know. What happened to him and how long has he been like this?" I look at her and just start sobbing.

"Kammie, it's complicated, Felix seems to be having some confidence issues these days, that's all. He will be fine, he loves me so much" I can see her shaking her head from side to side "Seriously, I'll be fine. Anyway tell me about you and Luca, you looked pretty close when I was leaving" I need to change the subject and get it off Felix.

"Tasha, I know what you are doing, but just so you know, I will be looking out for you and will be keeping an eye on Felix. Ok ok ok Luca is just everything I want in a man, he is gorgeous and he's very sensual, I think he likes me too. I went back to his place, but we never got chance for anything to happen as he got a call from Felix and we both rushed over to be with you" she tightens her grip on my hand." I went back to his after we left the hospital, they wouldn't let us in to see you, he held me while I cried all the way home and then he cuddled me all night. I needed some reassurance that you were ok Tasha, I was scared" she lets a tear fall out of her eye.

"Kammie it's ok, I'm going to be fine. I'm going to be resting for a few days and then I'll be back on track. Anyway, you and Luca are coming over for dinner this evening, you'll see everything is fine" I smile at her because I need her to know that I will be fine, that me and Felix will be fine, that everything will be fine.

We sit and chat about Luca for a while and then Kammie gets up to leave "I'm going before Felix shows up to take you home", she kisses me on the head and then walks out the door. I lay there thinking about our conversation and then start to drift off.

After a good nap I wake to see Felix standing over my bed, smiling at me. "Tasha, you look so much better after a sleep. Now, I have made arrangements for Kammie and Luca to spend some time looking after you this week when I can't babe, you'll be well looked after" he takes my hand and lifts it to his mouth and kisses it.

"What time is the doctor coming in Tasha, I just want to get you home, so you can start to get better" he says sitting on the side of the bed. "I think I'll go out and see if I can find him" he stands and walks out of the room.

The door opens and the doctor comes in with his paperwork ready to be signed. "Hi Natasha, how are you feeling now? You were sleeping when I came in earlier" he walks up to the bed and starts checking my vital signs. He's writing things down as he goes around the bed." I feel ok, I'm still tired, my ribs and my head hurt but I just want to get home doctor" I say hoping he will sign the paperwork and let me go home.

"Natasha, I'm happy enough for you to go home, I just need you to sign the paperwork and then I can give you your follow up paperwork. I'll give you a prescription for strong pain killers and some sleeping tablets, and then I want you to come back on Friday into outpatients so that I can check up on your ribs. There's also some numbers with the prescription just in case you need to change your appointment" he says looking at me with eyes wide open as if to say "you know which numbers I'm talking about".

"Thank you doctor, I will be back on Friday for my check up" I smile, I can't believe I can go home, I'm happy to be leaving here but anxious about being at home, does that make sense?

I take the numbers off the doctor and hide them with my prescription in my bag. He gave me enough tablets to last until tomorrow so I don't need to go to the pharmacy until then.

Felix helps me to put my stuff together and then he takes my hand and helps me to the car. On the drive home, Felix holds my hand the whole time and he is rubbing my hand with his thumb, he is talking about dinner and what he is going to cook.

When we get to the house, he carries my bag and holds my hand, once inside he walks me over to the couch and makes me sit down, he grabs the blanket he has left there and gives it to me.

"Felix I'm fine honestly don't fuss around me" I say looking at him. "If you want to do something for me I'd love a cup of tea" I smile at him.

"No problem babe, coming right up, anything for you" he leans forward and kisses my forehead "Glad to have you home Tasha, I love you" he walks off into the kitchen.

I MUST HAVE DOZED OFF again because the next thing I know Kammie is kneeled down in front of me smiling at me "Hi sleepyhead, how are you feeling?"

I smile back at her " I feel fine Kammie it's just a bit sore when I laugh so don't make any jokes at dinner time" I can feel a chuckle coming on, I hope I manage to hold it in.

"Ok fine, I promise" Kammie says smiling holding her hand out to me to help me get up.

I take her hand and she pulls me up gently and we link arms and walk into the kitchen. Luca comes over and hugs me very gently, "hey hun, how are you feeling? We were worried about you! You look better than you did last night."

I smile weakly "Thanks Luca, I know what you did for me, thank you". I kiss him on the cheek.

The smell in the kitchen is gorgeous and I walk over to see what is cooking, it's my favourite - roast beef. Who knew Felix could cook? "Dinner's going to be 10 minutes babe, why don't you take a seat and relax" he says looking at Luca strangely.

I sit at the table and Kammie joins me, we chat about work and then I remember I have two second interviews this week. What am I going to? Will I be able to make the interviews as they don't take a lot of movement and then I can come home and rest for the remainder of the week. I decide to broach the subject during dinner and see what everyone's reaction is. It's not long before Felix is telling Luca to sit at the table and he starts to bring dinner over.

I notice he has given everyone wine except me, but he has given me a wine glass with sparkling water in it. I presume that is because of the medication and I look at Felix and smile. He smiles back.

Dinner is delicious and not much is said while everyone eats. I've finished my dinner so I say "Felix that was absolutely delicious, I didn't know you could cook like this, I'll have to let you make dinner more often" I laugh very gently because it hurts, the painkillers must be wearing off.

"Babe, you always cook much nicer food than I do, which is why I don't do it very often" he smiles at me, I think he is happy that I complimented him.

"I need to ask you all something" I say and they all look at me expectantly. "I have two interviews scheduled for Monday and Tuesday, they are second round interviews and I don't want to put them off. Do you think I should go or should I ring them and postpone?" I sit there looking at them trying to see what they are thinking.

"Well, I know this is important to you Tasha, but

only you can tell if you are feeling up to it or not" Kammie says. She always likes to sit on the fence.

"Tasha, I know you won't go if you don't feel 100%, so I would say see how you feel in the morning, you might not be so sore after another day and night of pain medication" Luca says smiling at me.

"Babe, don't feel you have to go I'm sure if you ring them and explain they will understand, but I do think that Luca is right. See how you feel tomorrow" Felix says as he looks down at his wine glass. I know he is only saying that to make me happy, he hasn't really been enthusiastic about me looking for another job.

"I think you're all right, only I can tell if I feel up to it and maybe I should wait until the morning to see if I'm ok. I can always ring them tomorrow morning if I don't feel up to it. I don't really want to let them down and I was excited about both jobs." Yeah I think I'll wait til the morning. Thank you for coming over tonight, it means the world to me, it really does, I'm sorry if I gave you all a fright, I promise to be more careful in future" I look at each one of them when I say that.

Luca looks down the table at me and says "OK, well I'm on duty tomorrow morning so I'll come over early and I can drive you to the interview if you want to go, if not then we can just hang here. Ok Tasha?"

"Thanks Luca, I appreciate it" I smile at him, he really is a lovely guy and I hope that him and Kammie get together, I know me and Felix told them to stay away from each other because they were both players, but I can see how much they like each other and it's different now we are married. It would be perfect if they got together, just how I like things to be, perfect!

Luca and Felix stand up and start to clear away the dishes "Come on Tasha, let's go in the lounge and leave the guys to clear up" Kammie says helping me out of the chair. It still hurts when I stand up. Will I be able to carry this off at an interview, I'm not sure I will.

We sit on the couch when we get into the lounge, Kammie puts one leg under her and turns to face me, with her arm along the back of the couch. "That dinner was fabulous Tasha you should let Felix cook more often" she chuckles when she says this. "Now Tasha, how are you feeling? Does it still hurt? Do you need some painkillers now you've eaten?"

"Whoa that's a lot of questions Kammie! Yes it still hurts! Yes I do need some more painkillers! And no I don't need you to get them for me before you ask" I wink at her and turn around slowly to find my handbag, it's on the floor and I try to bend over to get into it but the pain is too bad. I sit back upright again and look at Kammie "Well, actually I do need you to get them for me apparently."

She smiles at me "Ok Miss Independent I will" she gets off the couch and goes to my bag for the tablets "There's a lot of paperwork in here, is this what the doctor gave you? Can I do anything with it?"

I reach out and I almost shout "No! Just leave that alone Kammie, I can look after that myself" she stops and looks at me strangely "OK if you're sure" she says as she hands me my tablets and sits back down.

"Sorry Kammie, it's just so painful but I don't want Felix to know how bad it is because he won't let me go to these interviews otherwise and I really need a new job" I say hoping that she will believe that story.

"Hmmm, ok Tasha, but if you need me to go to the pharmacy tomorrow then just ask. When are you back at the hospital for a check up?" she asks.

"Friday, the doctor wants to see how I get on with a week of rest and he can work out my treatment plan then" I sigh." Let's change the subject. Did you spend time with Luca today or did you just arrive together? Is anything happening that I need to be excited about?" I smile because I want her to be happy.

"Well, after the hospital I went back to his house to give him an update and then we went out for coffee before we came over here. We are sharing a cab home, so who knows. I really like him though Tasha, I always have done, I think he's out of my league, but I won't know if I don't try" she laughs.

"I think you make a great couple, Luca is a really good guy, I'm going to ask him his intentions tomorrow" I laugh.

"No way, no you're not" she laughs." So tell me about these interviews, why are they so important to you?"

"The one tomorrow is for Clifton Associates, they are a Facilities Company who have lots of premises, but they are all here in Bristol so I won't have to travel and stay overnight. I don't want to be away from Felix anymore, now that we are married." I stop for a moment to think about what I just said. "The one on Tuesday is for Blue Eye, a Marketing Company and it's with the HR Manager and the Operations Director. I like both jobs and they would both prove a challenge, but if I had to choose one, then I would definitely want the second one" I smile because I know that I have to work hard to get either one of them, but that seems exciting to me.

"They both sound good Tasha, good luck with either of them. I know you will get the one you want" she smiles at me and then she gets up and gives me a hug "I love you Tasha I really do, but you would tell me if something was going on wouldn't you" She's rubbing my back and I know she expects me to answer her.

"Nothing is going on, what do you mean Kammie?" I'm hoping that by playing the innocent will work in my favour this time.

"OK Tasha if that's how you want to play it that's fine, just know that I'm here for you anytime of the day or night. That goes for Luca too you know!" She moves back to look me in the eyes.

"Thanks Kammie I know you are and Luca is Felix's friend but I know he is there for me too" I smile "I'm getting tired now and I need to be up early in the morning, I might take some of the sleeping tablets and pain relief and go to bed. I'm going in the kitchen to tell the lads, is that ok?" I make to stand up, but it hurts and Kammie stands up and helps me up.

"Are you sure you'll be ok in the morning Tasha?" she asks looking concerned." Yeah I'll be fine honest, I need to do this Kammie" I say standing up straight and walking towards the kitchen.

"Hi guys, I'm going to go to bed, take some sleeping tablets and pain relief and try and get a good nights sleep before my interview tomorrow. This weekend seems like it has been very long" I look at Felix and say "night". "Luca, I need to be at my interview for 8.00 in the morning, are you sure you'll be able to take me for that time?"

Luca smiles at me "Of course I will Tasha, I hope Felix can dress you though, I don't want to have to do that for you" he winks at me.

"Yes I'm capable of doing that thanks Luca" Felix says giving him a punch on the arm "You don't need to help my wife with that".

"Oh god, no thanks Luca, no disrespect" I laugh gently. I walk over to Felix and lean up to kiss him on the lips, he gently puts his arms around me and pulls me into a hug. He kisses me very gently and then pulls back and says "Night babe, I'll be up as soon as I can, hope you sleep well".

"Night everyone, see you tomorrow Luca, see you soon Kammie" I turn and start to walk up the stairs, get undressed which hurts and then slide into bed. It's like every time I hurt it reminds me of what happened, I don't like to remember it, I just want to forget it and move on and go back to my perfect life. I take my tablets, swallow them, lie down and then I fall asleep really quickly.

10

THE NEXT MORNING, Felix wakes me up with a kiss on the forehead, "wake up babe its time to get ready".

I groan because I feel a bit sluggish after the sleeping tablets and then smile because I know I'm going for my interview this morning. I slowly get out of bed, trying not to hurt my ribs, and then I see Felix standing at the end of the bed with only his shorts on, smiling." Morning babe, how are the ribs today? Do you think you'll be able to manage the interview this morning?"

"I'm a little bit stiff and sore but I'll be fine, I'll take some pain relief and it'll only be for a short period of time" I smile at him.

"Ok, well if you go and put your make up on I'll get your clothes out and help you to get dressed" he turns to go to my wardrobe.

He is being very helpful and I feel protected and safe. I go into the bathroom and get myself ready, when I come out Felix is already dressed, looking very sexy in his navy blue suit. "I got your navy blue trouser suit with the peach blouse, it always looks so nice on you" he holds the blouse up to show me.

"Thanks Felix, I appreciate it, can you help me into them" I reach out for the underwear he has laid out for me, my baby pink bra and matching panties.

He laughs "I don't normally help you into these babe, I normally help you out of them" he has such a sexy smile.

I laugh too and then lean against him and give him a slow kiss "Don't make me laugh, it hurts" He helps me step into them and then he does my bra up for me. He holds my trousers while I step into them and then I can do the blouse up myself. I realise that the blouse is a high neck, but I don't say anything. I brush my hair and Felix helps me with my jacket and my shoes. I look in the mirror and you wouldn't know that I had a couple of broken ribs. I also notice that the high neck on the blouse covers the fading bruises on my neck, which I now realise no one mentioned yesterday.

I get to the bottom of the stairs when the doorbell rings and Luca is stood there. He smiles when I open the door "Your chariot awaits mam" he laughs.

I turn and see Felix at the top of the stairs, he is looking at me strangely, don't tell me he's jealous of Luca, as far as I'm concerned Luca is like a brother to me, he is goddamn sexy, but he's a friend and that's all!

"I'll ring you after the interview Felix and Luca will bring me straight home ok. Love you" I say looking up the stairs.

"Good luck babe, yeah ring me after and let me know how you get on" he says and then turns to go back into the bedroom.

Luca helps me get into his car and as soon as he gets into the driver's side, I can feel an awkwardness between us that I've never detected before.

"How are you feeling Tasha? And I mean really feeling?" he asks and I can see him looking at me out of the corner of his eye.

"I've felt better to be honest Luca, but I'll be fine in a few days or so" I hope he believes me. I might be physically better, but mentally I'm not so sure!

"Tasha, can I ask you something? And will you tell me the truth?" he's really nervous and he's tapping the steering wheel while he's talking to me.

"Luca please, I don't need this right now, I'm going for an interview and I need my head to be in the right place. Can we talk after the interview, please? I'll answer your questions then" I look at him pleading him with my eyes to drop the subject.

"Ok, but when I'm looking after you this afternoon, then we talk!" he says.

"Fine, just get me to this interview on time" I laugh.

He pulls up outside the building and says "Right Tasha, I'm going to park the car and wait for you in The Cozy Place Coffee Shop over the road, when you've finished your interview come and find me in there, ok"

"Ok and Luca, thanks again" I say and peck him on the cheek and then turn to walk into my interview.

I introduce myself to the receptionist and she asks me to wait. I feel really nervous, but that's only because I would love this job. I wait and then I'm brought into a room by the HR Manager and introduced to Mr Wolfe, the Operations Director.

He is in his late 30's and quite good looking, but he

comes across quite arrogant, I'm not sure I like him, but I don't let that deter me.

When the interview is over I walk across the road to meet Luca, I'm a little disappointed that I didn't click with Mr Wolfe but I'm still excited about the job prospect. Luca sees me coming in the door and stands to go to the till to order me a coffee "What do you want Tasha?" he asks.

"A one shot skinny latte please" I say going to sit at the table Luca was sat at.

He comes back with my coffee and sits down, I take a good swig and sit looking at him "So, how did it go? Tell me about it" he asks.

"Well it went really well. I was able to answer all the questions and give good examples of Facilities Management, the only thing was I didn't feel I clicked with Mr Wolfe, he seemed very distant but at the same time he seemed very interested in me" I say, it was strange though because he wanted to know about my personal life.

"Mr Wolfe? Did you get his first name?" he asks me

"That's a strange question Luca, but yes his name is Douglas" I look at him because it's a weird question.

"Was he our age, dark hair, quite short?" he asks.

"Yeah, do you know him?" I ask.

"Yeah. Me and Felix went to school with him, he's a bit arrogant but he's a nice guy, you could work for a lot worse" he smiles.

"Ah I see. Felix said he knew someone in the company, why didn't he tell me it was Douglas when I said I have an interview with Mr Wolfe? Mind you nothing surprises me anymore" I laugh a little from being nervous.

"I don't know why he didn't tell you, that's very strange. As for things being weird lately, yeah that's something I want to talk to you about Tasha, I know you don't want to talk about it so I'm going to say what I think and then you can decide to talk if you want. Ok?" Luca is looking me right in the eye and I know he expects me to say something but I can't, my heart is racing so much, so all I can do is nod my head.

Luca clears his throat and takes a sip of his coffee " I've noticed that Felix isn't himself these days, particularly where you're concerned. I don't know why he's being like that considering you're now married. It's like he's worried you're going to leave him or something. He doesn't want to go out anymore when I ask him and you know what party animals we all were. I saw what was going on in Jesters on Saturday night, I saw you trip and I saw your drink falling on that guy, I told him all of that but I have never seen him react like he did. Is there anything going on that would make him think you'd cheat on him?" I'm sitting there and I can feel tears welling up in my eyes, I can't speak so I just shake my head.

Luca continues "Tasha I need to ask you what happened when you got home Saturday night. I saw you laid at the bottom of the stairs and you were in and out of consciousness, I thought at one stage you were dead" he reaches across the table and covers my hands, rubbing them to comfort me "I also saw the marks on your neck, because I examined you and thought you had twisted or broken it. I didn't say anything to Felix because I was in shock. Did he do that to you? Did you really fall down the stairs? Tasha talk to me, you need to talk to someone" he removes his hands from mine and sits back in his chair. He slowly rubs his chin as if he's thinking.

I really don't know what to say and Luca is Felix's friend so I need to be careful what I do say to him. Would he believe me? Well from what he just said I think he would, can I risk it? I'm not sure. "Luca some things are private and should be kept private, I'm sure Felix wouldn't like me talking to you about any of this" his eyebrows shoot up.

"Are you serious Tasha? I'm trying to help you out and talk to you, I know I'm Felix's friend, but I care for you and no man should lay a finger on a woman. EVER!" he shouts the last word and people are looking at us.

"Luca stop shouting please" I say crying. I flinch and sink lower in my chair, I can't believe how Luca's shouting has affected me.

"Tasha I'm sorry, I'm sorry but I know something happened on Saturday night and I know you're hiding it from me and I don't understand why. If Felix needs help then we can get him help" he says calming down.

"NO! You can't tell Felix we had this conversation Luca, please" I'm begging him now and I grab his hands across the table "Please"

"I won't say anything to him about our conversations ever, but I will be asking him exactly what happened. As his friend he would expect no less from me. What I don't want is for something to be going on and you not telling me or Kammie and then something really bad happening. What would have happened Saturday if he hadn't rung us? He didn't want to ring for an ambulance, I had to do it Tasha. I can't even start thinking about it because I just want to bloody kill him! I know you're not going to tell me, but I can work out myself what happened. Can you answer me one question. Is this the first time? Tasha look at me, I need to see your eyes when you answer the question".

I sit there looking at the table, what do I do now? What do I say? I can feel Luca looking at me, waiting for me to say something. I slowly lift my head and look into his eyes "No it's not".

Luca stands up and puts his hands in his hair and shouts out "Fuck", everyone is looking at us again, I'm sure we will be asked to leave soon.

"Luca please sit down. I'm sure it will be the last time, we were drunk on Saturday night and it just went too far, it was kind of an accident honestly. I was going too fast down the stairs Luca, he reached out to grab me and I slipped, you have to believe me. Please you can't say anything to Felix, I don't know how he'll react" now I'm really sobbing.

"Sorry Tasha, I didn't mean to shout I was hoping you were going to say yes it was the first time. Fuck. We need to leave, I need to let off some steam and I can't do that in here. Come on honey let's go" he stands up and walks to my side of the table, where he holds out his hand to help me up as I'm still sore and the pain killers are starting to wear off. He puts his other hand on my lower back and gently guides me out of the coffee shop.

"The car is this way, come on are you ok? Are you in a lot of pain?" he asks looking down at me with so much concern in his eyes.

"I'm OK, I just need to take some pain killers that's

all, are you ok?" I ask, not really wanting an answer.

"No, I'm not really! I don't know what to say or what to do Tasha. Felix has been my best friend for years and I know he gets jealous but I would never have put him down as someone who could touch a woman like that. It makes me sick. I know that I won't be able to look at him when I see him. I'm going to have to make sure I'm out the house before he comes home". We've reached the car and Luca opens the door for me, when I have my seatbelt on he closes the door and starts to walk around the other side. I hear a lot of swearing and I feel the car move, he's obviously kicked the car or something. He then opens the door and climbs in, "Sorry about that Tasha I just need to scream out loud for a minute, now let's get you home so we can watch some movies and have lunch, what do you say?"

"Luca that sounds like the best thing I've heard all day" I smile and he drives me home.

We spend the afternoon watching silly movies, laughing and I sleep for a while too. At about 5.00pm Luca says "Tasha I'm going to go home, I don't want to be here when Felix gets home, are you ok with that?" I nod my head and say "I am and promise me you won't ever mention it to him, please?"

"I don't know if I can make that promise, I can however promise that I'll never say you told me, but I do have a mind of my own and can make my own conclusions. I will be keeping a good eye on him from now on" he stands up from the couch "Now do you need anything before I go? Drink? Food?"

"No Luca I'm fine thanks. Felix will be home soon and I'm sure he will look after me" I say. I hear him say something under his breath but I ignore it.

"I'm taking you to another interview tomorrow aren't I? Is it the same time?"

"Yeah Luca I have to be there for 8.00am are you sure it's ok with you? I don't want to take advantage.

"Tasha it's fine honest, now you just relax and I'll see you in the morning honey ok" he leans forward and places a kiss on the top of my head and then he let's himself out.

I sit there thinking about today, about the interview, then I remember that I am supposed to be going to Plymouth tomorrow, so I ring the office and remind them so that they can send someone else. I think about the conversation with Luca and then this afternoon watching silly movies and I begin to realise I've enjoyed today, Luca is a good man. I forgot to ask him about Kammie, I'll do that tomorrow. I smile to myself.

Felix comes home about half an hour later, he walks in the door and comes straight over to me and kisses me "Hey babe how're you feeling? Where's Luca?"

"I'm ok thanks, I've had a good enough day, I haven't cooked dinner though, is that ok? Luca had to go about 20mins ago" I say putting my arms around his neck gently, because it hurts when I stretch "How was your day Felix?"

He kisses me again then stands up straight "Of course it's ok. I'm going to cook dinner for you, I thought Luca would be here, I was going to cook for him too. My day was ok, just you weren't there, so I missed you"

"Well if I get a new job I won't see you, but we will be able to have lunch together like dates" I smile at him sexily.

He laughs and turns away, I think I hear him say "that's what you think" but I can't be sure. He walks into the kitchen and I can hear the sounds of pots and pans and then I can smell something lovely. After about 15 minutes he comes back into the room and holds out his hand to me "Dinner is served Madame" he helps to slowly pull me up from the couch. I allow him to pull me behind him, although it reminds me a little of Saturday night, but I push that thought to the back of my head. When we walk into the kitchen I see that he's laid the table and it all looks so lovely and romantic.

"Oh Felix it looks lovely, thanks so much" I pull him to me and kiss him. I only kiss him gently on the lips, but it makes him smile.

"Anything for you Tasha, anything" he pulls my chair out for me to sit, this is the Felix I fell in love with and married.

We spend the evening talking about my interview, I mention Douglas a couple of times, but he never once said he knew him, strange! He seems keen on me getting this job, which pleases me. I tell him I have to wait to hear from HR to find about a third and final interview. Soon it's time for bed, Felix has washed all the dishes and cleaned the kitchen. He follows me up to bed with a drink for my tablets and helps me to get undressed and ready for bed. He rolls onto his side facing me when he gets into bed and he looks at me while he is rubbing my arm. "I love you so much Tasha, I really do. I don't know what I would do without you in my life" he leans over and kisses me hard, he is careful not to touch my ribs, I can feel his tongue trying to gain access to mine and I open my mouth slightly so they can meet.

He abruptly stops and kisses me gently on the lips "Sleep tight babe, sleep tight. I'll wake you for your interview"

"I love you Felix" I reply and I can feel myself drifting off.

11

THE NEXT MORNING RUNS like yesterday with Felix waking me, picking my clothes, dressing me and Luca showing up at the door when I'm ready to leave. He shouts "Hi" to Felix and then closes the door behind me.

"Come on honey let's go" Again he puts his hand on my lower back, somehow this makes me feel safe, he helps me in the car and then closes the door and goes around to his side." So where are we heading today Tasha" he asks

"I need to be at Blue Eye if that's ok" I say to him smiling. He's in a good mood today, hopefully we can get through it without talking about me and Felix.

"That's fine honey, now tell me about this job" he seems genuinely interested.

I spend the journey into the city telling Luca about the Administration Manager's job at Blue Eye. He asks some questions and the journey flies by. When we arrive he stops outside the building to drop me off and again looks around to see where we are then he remembers that

The Cozy Place Coffee Shop is a few minute walk, but I know where it is. "I'll be fine, I'll meet you there, I shouldn't be longer than an hour" I say getting out of the car.

"No problem, ring me if you need help Tasha and good luck". I say thanks and close the door. I stand up straight and take a deep breath, which instantly makes me groan from the pain, I hope I can make it through without anyone noticing my pain. It's not time for me to take my pills yet.

I go to reception and announce myself, I'm told to wait for a few minutes for the HR Manager and the Operations Director. I'm sitting there when this man walks towards the exit, oh my god is all I can think. He is gorgeous! Wow! I didn't think people like that existed, he is like a Greek god. He looks at me and smiles, he seems familiar like I've met him before but I just can't put my finger on it, he looks like he is going to say something but stops himself, instead he turns and walks back to reception. He talks to the receptionist and then turns to leave, as he's walking past me he stops and looks at me like he's double checking something. I can't quite place him, maybe he was going for an interview for the same job or something. I smile at him and nod my head. He smiles at me and I can't breathe, it feels like I've forgotten how to do a simple thing like breathe. He walks past me slowly, looking deep into my eyes as he goes past. It is only when he walks out the door that I remember how to breathe and blink. I can't help myself turning in my seat to watch him out of the window and I see him stride towards a car and as he opens the door he turns to look at me. I'm so embarrassed, I quickly turn away so he can't see me looking. I've never looked at another man like that, not even Felix, but then again I've never been affected by another man quite like I was just now.

While I'm waiting for Helen, the HR Manager my phone rings, it's not a number I recognise, but I answer it anyway "Hello, Tasha speaking"

A deep husky voice, which reverberates through my body, says "Hi my name is Caleb, you gave me your number on Saturday night" I'm trying to remember Saturday night, who is this and why did I give him my number?

"I'm sorry Saturday night was a difficult night for me, can you elaborate? I don't remember giving anyone my number" I say, I'm a little bit angry now, did I actually give someone my number? As I am saying this, I remember giving my number to the guy who I spilled my drink on, I don't say I remember him though.

"That's a shame that you don't remember me, I certainly remember you." He pauses and my mind is in overdrive. "In fact, I haven't stopped thinking about you. You tripped and spilled your drink on me and then you offered to pay for my dry cleaning" he says and I think he must be smiling because it sounds like he is.

"Oh my god, yes I remember now. I'm so embarrassed. Just let me know how much it is for the dry cleaning and I'll pay for it" what a klutz I am. I'm trying to remember what he looks like, but I can't piece it together. Anything that happened on Saturday night is overshadowed by what happened when I got home.

"It's ok it's all been dry cleaned. I think that maybe you should take me for a cup of coffee as payment instead" he says with a little chuckle.

"Erm, well, erm, I could do that but erm I'm married you see" why am I not just telling him a straight no, what has gotten into me. I feel really flustered, I can feel myself getting hotter by the minute.

"Ok, I didn't ask for a marital status! I only want a coffee, nothing else, honest. You owe me at least that" now he's definitely smiling, I can hear it in his voice.

"Ok, ok" I'm surprised at how easy I've given in, but I do feel guilty for spilling my drink on him. "This week is a bit difficult for me, I'm off work as I had a bit of an accident so I can't drive or walk far, but I should be able to have a coffee next week providing I'm back at work" I say, and I can feel my voice vibrating slightly because I'm really nervous.

"Are you OK? What happened? Were you badly hurt? God I wish I'd phoned before now! I hope you are ok" he sounds genuinely concerned and he doesn't even know me.

"I'm fine, just a couple of broken ribs, but I'm recovering well thank you" I say, and I can feel myself blushing. I have no idea why I'm blushing I'm only talking on the phone!

"I'll wait for coffee until you're ready" he pauses to think "I'd like to call you to see if you are getting better if that's ok? I know that might seem strange to you, but I hate to think I caused you any problems on Saturday night, I saw how you left the club!" What can I say to that? If I remember rightly he was gorgeous, but he was also the cause of what happened later.

"I don't know if that is a good thing Caleb, but I will arrange to meet for a coffee next week, hopefully. I never renege on a deal and I offered to pay for your dry cleaning so I'll do that" I smile to soften the blow slightly.

"OK Tasha, I'll ring you later in the week and we can make arrangements then." Again he pauses, it's like he is taking time to think. "I've got to go into a meeting now, but I just wanted to tell you that you look beautiful today" and then he hangs up.

I look around to see if anyone is looking at me. What the hell? Where is he? I wish I could remember what he looks like. When did he see me?

I see someone walking towards me and I look up and I see it is Helen, the HR Manager, "Hi Natasha, are you ready? The Operations Director is ready to see you now" I try to stand up without showing the pain I am in and shake her hand. I know I looked a bit awkward getting up from my chair, but I'm determined to get through this interview as I really want this job, I can just feel good vibes from the people here.

I follow her down to a meeting room, which has glass doors and walls so that you can see straight into it. There is a man sitting in the room and he is talking on his phone "OK I'll let you know, don't worry big man I'll take it easy on her", he hangs up the phone and then he stands and turns towards me as I walk in. I shake his hand and he says "Good morning Natasha, I'm Dillon, pleased to meet you, I've heard wonderful things about you" he gestures to the chair for me to sit down.

I sit down, so does Helen and then he sits down too. For the next hour, I get drilled on procedures, how I would handle situations and when it is all over, I'm drained. Dillon stands and offers his hand to shake mine,

I push the chair out and struggle to stand up. I'm stiff and my pain killers must be wearing off, it hurts, but I manage it by leaning on the table, so I stand and shake his hand.

He looks at me with great concern and asks "Are you OK Natasha? You've gone very pale!"

I really can't hide the pain and I have to hold onto the table to keep myself stable "I'm really sorry" I take a shallow breath in so as not to cause anymore pain. "I didn't want you to see me in pain. I had an accident on Saturday night and I broke a couple of ribs, but I really wanted to come to this interview because I am really interested in the position you have here" I can feel tears coming to the surface, I don't want Dillon or Helen to see them so I look to the floor.

"Oh my god Natasha! You should have cancelled the interview" he says coming over to me." He reaches out to touch me on the shoulder and I flinch, it wasn't intentional, I think it was because I was in pain. He pulls his hand back and looks at me "we would have understood" he says.

"I didn't want to cancel because I didn't want to let you down and I wanted to prove to myself that I could do it" I say and I'm so embarrassed. "I'm fine honestly, thank you so much for seeing me today, I really appreciate this opportunity" I start to walk towards the door.

"As long as you are ok to leave!" Dillon says.

I turn as I'm going through the door "Please don't hold this against me, I'm really interested in this job"

They both look at me and Dillon says "We won't, don't worry, not at all" I smile and turn away and start to walk to the exit.

12

WHEN I GET OUTSIDE of the building, I stop and lean back against the wall and start to cry. I don't know what I'm crying about, I just feel like crying. I think it's because I got caught out after the interview and also because I'm in pain. I take a few deep breaths and ring Luca, I need him to come and get me, I don't feel like I can walk a couple of blocks to meet him.

"Luca can you come and get me please, I can't walk to the coffee shop" I'm crying when I'm talking to him.

"Tasha what's wrong? Why are you crying honey" I can hear him opening the door to the coffee shop and starting to walk towards me. "I'm coming Tasha, just stay where you are. I'll be there in a few minutes ok, stay on the phone and talk to me, tell me about your interview, how did it go?" he's trying to calm me down, trying to get me to talk about something "normal".

I just can't speak for some reason, it has been a very strange morning and I need some pain killers quick "I'm ok Luca, I just need some pain relief, I hurt myself standing up after the interview and I'm in pain, please just come and get me, I don't think I can stand for much longer" I'm sobbing.

I can feel myself sliding down the wall when I see Luca running towards me, he catches me just before I fall to the ground. Why am I reacting like this? I don't know what's happening to me. I can feel Luca's arms around me and I lean into him sobbing "I'm here Tasha, I'm here, come on just let it all out" He holds me for about 10 minutes as I just cry. I finally stop crying and then I stand back and look at Luca. I'm really embarrassed.

"I'm sorry Luca, I don't know what happened. I stood up after the interview and I hurt myself and they saw me wince and asked me about it. I told them that I had broken ribs and they said I should have rearranged the meeting and then I just started panicking. "What if I've ruined my chances now? I really want this job Luca! By the time I got outside I realised how serious this all is and what could have happened to me on Saturday night and I haven't even told my Mum and Dad because I don't know how to explain it all to them." I take a deep breathe, I can feel myself getting hysterical. "Luca, can you take me to my Mum's, I think I need to talk to them and tell them. Firstly, I need a drink to take my pain killers with. I really need to take them before I go there and talk to them"

"Tasha, of course I'll take you to your Mum's. Come on there's a shop over here, we'll get you a drink and then we'll go to the car and drive to your Mum's" He says taking me by the arm and walking slowly with me to the shop.

We are in the car on the way to my Mum's when

Luca asks "What are you going to say to your parents Tasha?" This is the question I've been dreading, I don't know what to say to them, they wouldn't believe me if I told them the truth, I don't think I believe the truth!

"I've always been clumsy they'll understand when I say that I fell down the stairs. I just feel like everything is falling apart and I can't stop it. I'm sure I'll be fine I just need a Mummy hug!" I chuckle a little.

Luca doesn't say anything but drives to my parents, he helps me out of the car and puts his hand on my lower back to support me as I walk to the front door. I stop and take a deep breath, then I open the door and walk in." Mum, Dad, it's me" I yell to let them know I'm here.

Me and Luca walk into the house and Mum comes out to hug me, when she does I flinch because it hurts. She sees me flinch and asks me what happened, I explain to her that I fell down the stairs and hurt myself, she believes me because I am so clumsy.

"Mum, I'm not going back to work for over a week, I need to go for a check up on Friday to get the OK to go back to work. I need some help this week. I need YOU to help me, will you come and stay with me this week?" I ask her but I'm not sure she will as I have been so independent for so long, but she looks at me and hugs me gently.

"Tasha I will always be there for you as long as you need me even though you never need me. I'm so happy that you still need me baby girl" she kisses me on the cheek "I'm going to get packed and talk to your Dad about this" with that she walks out the room. Luca looks at me and smiles.

While she talks to Dad and gets organised, my

phone rings and it's a strange number, I just know it's Caleb. I answer with trepidation and walk out the room.

"Tasha are you ok?" he sounds so worried "I heard.... I had a feeling you were in pain, is everything ok? I know you don't know me but after you told me about your accident I was worried about you" I can't believe what I'm hearing, who is this guy? Why is he so worried about me?

"I'm fine, I had a bad morning but you don't need to concern yourself Caleb, honestly! I'll ring you next week so I can take you for coffee, ok" I say, I'm touched that he is worried and is interested enough to check up on me, but I really don't need this complication in my life right now.

"That's fine Tasha, but I'll still worry about you, you looked so frail this morning, but yet so beautiful. I'll look forward to hearing from you for coffee" and he hangs up. Why does he keep doing that? Where the hell did he see me this morning, this day just keeps getting weirder! I save his number in my phone, so at least I will know his number to ring him for coffee!

I walk back into the kitchen and walk into Luca who is talking to my Mum "I'm really worried about her, Jean, she's trying to be strong, but I know she isn't really" My Mum nudges him to let him know I'm behind him, he turns and says "Tasha, you know I worry about you honey".

I smile at him, because I know he does, I walk over to him and hug him "Luca, you are a great friend and I love you, thanks" I have to walk back out of the room because I can feel the tears coming, again.

About 2pm we drive over to my house, we are all

very quiet in the car. Luca helps my Mum carry her bag into the house, while she helps me out of the car.

Luca makes us all a cup of tea and then leaves around 5pm, he knows that Felix is due home soon and he's not ready to see him yet.

I rang Felix to tell him that Mum is coming to stay. He wasn't overly happy! I'm not sure why, because he gets on with both Mum and Dad.

Felix arrives home and comes into the lounge, he gives me a kiss and gives my Mum a hug." Jean, I'm glad you're here, Tasha needs some looking after. She's been busy with her interviews during the last couple of days, it's taken her mind off things but she's not got anything planned now. She has a check up on Friday, that's it. Can I smell dinner? Something smells nice" he says sniffing the air!

"Yes, Felix I cooked something, I hope you don't mind" Mum says and I know that she's cooked his favourite.

She disappears into the kitchen and I can hear her laying the table. "How are you feeling babe?" Felix says.

"I'm ok, but I hurt myself after my interview and I got a little bit upset, but I'm ok now" I say.

He leans down to kiss me again and before he reaches my lips he snarls "I can't believe you asked your Mum to come and stay here! Did you tell her what happened? Did you Tasha?"

Did I just hear him right? Is he admitting that he pushed me down the stairs? I didn't think he would ever do that!

"Felix I told her that I fell down the stairs because I was drunk, that's what happened ok" I can feel myself getting mad now. "What is wrong with you?"

"There is nothing wrong with me Tasha, I'm just making sure you don't start lying to people that's all" he starts to walk out of the room.

"What are you talking about Felix, I fell down the stairs because I was drunk and that's what I've told everyone" I can't deal with him right now, so I pull myself up off the couch and walk past him into the kitchen.

Dinner is lovely and Felix is the perfect host, Mum would never have guessed there was anything wrong in my perfect marriage.

After dinner I say "I'm off to bed, I'm tired, I don't have to be up early so I hope I have a good sleep" I walk over to Mum and give her a hug and a quick kiss and then do the same to Felix.

I turn and go upstairs to get ready for bed, I'm just about to turn my phone off when it sounds to let me know I have a text message. It's from Caleb, what does he want at this time of night? What if Felix sees it? I'm panicking now! I need to tell him not to keep texting me, it will only make things worse with Felix.

"I'm sorry to text so late but I wanted to make sure you were OK! I saw you this morning outside Blue Eye, I saw you sliding down the wall. You looked very upset"

I start feeling warm inside that this person I don't know is so interested in me and seems to care so much about me that they would text me to see how I am. I smile to myself. I really need to tell him to stop texting me though.

"Caleb, thank you for being concerned about me, I really appreciate it. I had a really bad morning and I hurt my ribs. Then all my emotions caught up with me"

"I feel like I need to look after you and I don't know why? This feels really strange Tasha, it's like fate intervened on Saturday night and introduced us. You fell into my life like an Angel coming to rescue me, I feel like I need to have you in my life, I can't explain it any better than that."

Wow, this is moving in a direction I hadn't thought of. Just tell him Tasha, tell him to stop texting you! I can't! I want to know what he has to say.

"Caleb, I don't even know anything about you and I'm not sure I should. As for fate, I wish I hadn't tripped and spilled my drink on you, because I wouldn't be in so much pain now"

"Did you hurt yourself when you fell into my life? I thought you had an accident?"

"No, I hurt myself later, but if I hadn't tripped and talked to you, I wouldn't have argued with Felix, my husband, and I wouldn't have fallen down the stairs"

"I can see why you wished you hadn't met me, but let me tell you that fate had it planned anyway and we will meet again, soon, very soon Tasha"

"What do you mean?"

"You'll see when the day comes, now go to sleep my beautiful Angel.Sweet dreams, I'll wait for coffee"

"Night Caleb"

Why is he texting me? What does he mean "fate intervened anyway"? I lay in bed thinking about Caleb, he seems to care or is he just screwing with my mind. I try to picture him but my mind is a bit fuzzy from the tablets and from being drunk when I met him. I know I should have told him not to text me, what if Felix finds out? I can't believe I have to worry about Felix finding my phone. I should have told him not to text me. Next time! I delete his messages just in case!

I slowly drift off and have an erotic dream of a faceless man, who is looking after me and whispering in my ear "I love you Tasha, I'll take care of you."

13

I WAKE TO FIND Felix getting dressed for work "Morning Felix" I say drowsily.

"Morning Tasha, I hope you take it easy today, you've got your check up on Friday, you want to make sure you'll be well healed by then". He comes over and kisses me and whispers in my ear "I hope your Mum isn't staying too long Tasha"

What!! "Why? She's here to look after me" I say trying to sit up.

"That's my job. I'm your husband!" he seems angry and I don't want Mum hearing him raise his voice at me.

"OK Felix I'll suggest she goes home tomorrow, but if I know Mum she won't go until after my check up on Friday".

"Just convince her!" he walks into the bathroom and I stare after him. He's never had a problem with my Mum before.

When he walks out of the bathroom I still can't believe what he said. "Close your mouth Tasha it doesn't suit you, unless you want my cock in there" he starts coming towards me. Did he really just say that? I close my mouth anyway, that's the last thing I feel like.

"Shame I was just thinking about how it would be to have your mouth around my cock. Actually, open your mouth again Tasha" he's still coming towards me and he's opened his zip and pulled his cock out, it's big, hard and angry looking. I open my mouth and he slides it in. I try to protest but he just grabs the back of my head and starts to thrust his cock in and out of my mouth.

"Tasha oh my god that's so good, you were always good at blow jobs, who taught you?" he slams his cock to the back of my throat and I start to gag "How many men have you done this to?" he pulls it out and slams it back in, it hurts it's so far back in my throat and I'm not in the right position to open my throat to take all of him, I have tears falling down my face, it's hurting my ribs because I'm twisted in the bed. "You're a slut that's what you are" he rams his cock back in again, harder than the other times and I can feel myself start to gag "Take everything you slut" he says as he spurts his cum down my throat. He starts to slide his cock out of my mouth and then turns and walks back into the bathroom.

When he comes back he gets his shoes on and at the door he turns and says "Don't forget what I said about your Mum Tasha, sooner rather than later" and he walks through the door and closes it. I start sobbing quietly because I don't want Mum to hear me. What has happened to the man I married, why does he seem to hate me?

I can't believe how he has changed, why does he hate me so much? I thought he loved me. He's changing in front of my eyes and he's scaring me. When will this stop?

I pick up my phone when I've finished sobbing, I don't know why I do what I do next but I need someone to confide in, someone who doesn't know Felix, someone who will listen to me when I talk. So I send a text.

"Morning Caleb, I feel like I can talk to you when I can talk to no one else. Can I ask you a question?"

"Morning Tasha. You just made me very happy by saying that to me. You can ask anything. Fire away!"

"Are you or have you ever been married?"

"No I'm not and no I never have. Why?"

"I wanted to know if you thought it was right for a man to get married and then totally change almost overnight. Is this normal?"

"I don't know Tasha, but I know I wouldn't change who I am for a woman, you either love me or you don't. Be more specific and I'll see if I can help you"

"I just wondered if a man thought that when he got married he could have sex anytime, anywhere, with or without consent"

He doesn't reply straight away and I think maybe I've done something wrong, maybe I shouldn't have asked that question, it's very personal.

Caleb, I'm sorry just forget I asked"

"Sorry Tasha I was just trying to understand your question. Are you telling me what I think you're telling me?"

"I'm sorry I shouldn't have said anything Caleb, just ignore I said anything. I have to go my Mum is waiting

for me"

"Trying to change the subject Tasha? Ok just remember I'm here if you need someone to talk to. I'll always be available for you"

"Thanks Caleb, I don't know why I feel I can talk to you about this, but maybe it's because you are a stranger to me"

"I don't want us to be strangers for ever Tasha, but fate will intervene. I hope your day gets better Tasha"

"Thanks Caleb, have a good day doing whatever it is you do"

I climb out of the bed, delete his messages and put my phone in my pocket and start to make my way down the stairs. I can hear Mum in the kitchen making coffee, she is humming along to the radio.

"Hi Mum, how did you sleep?" I ask as I walk into the kitchen.

She turns to look at me, "Very well, although it was strange sleeping without your father" she smile at me "How about you sweetheart?"

"I slept well too, I think the fact that I knew I didn't have to get up early meant I had a good nights sleep. I think Kammie is coming over today to keep us company"

"Great, I love her, she keeps me laughing" Mum says smiling. "Now, will you show me your bruising sweetheart so that I can rub some arnica on it. I know you don't like my homeopathic remedies, but it will help the bruising to go down quicker"

"I'd like that, I hate looking at it. It reminds me of my accident and how clumsy I am" I say turning to go and help myself some coffee.

"Yeah you have always been clumsy Tasha, I can name at least 50 situations that you dropped things or fell over." She laughs as she starts to recall them "I don't remember you falling down the stairs before though."

We sit reminiscing for a couple of hours, we eat breakfast and drink loads of coffee while we chat.

Before we know it there is a knock at the door and Kammie lets herself in. She just walks in all the time, it's as if she lives here.

"Hey Tasha are you up and decent?" she walks into the kitchen before I have time to get up and go and meet her." Hey Jean, how are you, its good to see you" she walks over and kisses Mum on the cheek.

"Hey Kammie, how are you? How's your love life? Come tell me some of your dating stories, they always make me laugh" Mum says.

"Thanks Jean, I don't know whether to take that as a compliment or not" Kammie laughs.

We spend the next couple of hours laughing along with Kammie as she tells Mum her dating stories. We don't see the time passing us by, then before we know it its 4pm.Kammie jumps up and says "I have to go I'm meeting Luca for a drink" she winks at me.

I sit there with my mouth open and then I start to smile "We haven't finished this conversation and tomorrow we will have this conversation again and we will start with Luca, we need to know everything. Don't we Mum?"

"Oh yes girly, tell us everything tomorrow. Oh I can't wait to hear this gossip, Luca is one hot dude" me and Kammie both turn our heads abruptly to look at Mum and then the three of us burst out laughing.

"Don't get up Tasha, I'll let myself out. Jean I'll see you tomorrow and let the gossiping commence." She stands up and walks out of the kitchen and then out of the house.

When Kammie has gone, me and Mum go into the lounge and sit down "I haven't laughed like that for ages Tasha it was good fun" Mum says smiling at me. "How are you feeling baby girl?"

"I'm OK Mum, the pain isn't so bad now and if I keep on top of my tablets then it keeps the pain away. I've got my check up on Friday and I'm hoping to go to work on Monday" I say.

"Well fingers crossed they say you can" she stands up and starts walking into the kitchen "I'm going to make dinner, will you come keep me company?"

I nod and stand up to follow her. I get the feeling she wants to say something "Mum are you ok?" I touch her on her arm.

"Yeah I am, I just don't like to see you in pain, you look so unhappy and I want that pain to go away. I love you and don't want to see you suffer. Is Felix looking after you?" She asks and turns towards the fridge.

Thank god she can't see me because I visibly flinch and hold the countertop. "Of course he is, he loves me and is very good at looking after me" I try to smile while I say this.

"Good, he's a good man Tasha you'd be wise to hold onto him" she busies herself in the fridge getting out food for dinner. I know if Mum knew the truth she would take me out of the house and never make me come back but I know she wouldn't believe me, he's perfect in everyone's eyes.

After Felix comes home we have dinner and then we all sit down to watch TV. "So what are your plans for the rest of the week Jean?" Felix asks looking at me.

"Well I'm going with Tasha to her check up on Friday and then if the doctor says she can go back to work then I'll go home. Are you looking forward to having her on your own Felix?" She winks at him.

"Yes, I want to look after her like a good husband should" he smiles so sweetly I think I want to vomit. Everything he says these days has a hidden meaning meant especially for me. I am starting to hate being on my own with him, he's making my skin crawl, but then when he is being nice to me I love him so much. I'm confused!

The rest of the evening passes without incident and then we go to bed. Felix doesn't say anything about Mum but just kisses me goodnight as always.

14

IN THE MORNING I wake up after he has left. After what happened yesterday morning, I'm quite happy he's gone when I wake up. I turn my phone on and I see I have a text, it's from Caleb. I get excited opening it.

"Morning Tasha. How are you feeling? I didn't hear from you yesterday so I left you alone but I just needed to know you're ok"

"Morning Caleb. I feel a bit better today, I'm not as stiff and sore. I have a check up in the morning and I'm hoping to go back to work on Monday"

"That's great. How are things at home? Any better?"

"Nothing much going on but my Mum is here until the weekend. What have you been up to this week Caleb? Anything exciting which can take my mind off me!" I want to move away from the subject of me and Felix.

"Well other than having you fall into my life and totally upending it, my week has been pretty boring. Lots

of meetings, evening functions and a lot of thinking about you. Especially after yesterday! Are you sure you're ok?"

"Lots of evening functions sounds like fun not work!"

"Believe me Angel it's not fun being nice to people all night when you don't want to be there"

Did he just call me "Angel" I like it!

"You must have a good job if you're schmoozing all week lol"

"You could say that, it'd be more fun if you were going with me. Sorry I know that's inappropriate but it would definitely be more fun!"

I know I should tell him now! Tell him to stop texting me. Felix would probably kill me if he saw him texting me. Go on Tasha, tell him!

"Now, now Caleb! Are you working right now? Where are you?"

"Changing the subject again I see! Yeah I'm sat in my office, it's on the top floor and I'm looking out over Bristol City Centre. It's gorgeous. What about you Tasha?"

"I'm laid in bed getting the energy to get up and start my day"

"Wow! I'd say that view is better than mine any day. You shouldn't tell me you're laid in bed, that's hard for me to hear and not picture. What are you doing to me?"

"Sorry I didn't think about it like that. I'm laid in bed with 10 layers of clothes on and a face pack on ha

ha. Is that better?"

"Ha ha no! Now I can only imagine it's like pass the parcel peeling off a layer at a time lol"

"Ok stop! Get that picture out of your mind, I can't talk to you if you start picturing things like that" Go on Tasha, just say it to him!

"Sorry Tasha but to me you look like an angel sent down to tempt me"

What can I say to that. I don't know how to respond. Should I really be encouraging him to send me these messages. On the other hand it makes me feel better and puts a smile on my face.

"Tasha sorry did I scare you by saying that. I promise to restrain myself, please talk to me"

"Caleb you embarrassed me there and I was thinking maybe I shouldn't encourage you, maybe you shouldn't be sending me messages, but they make me feel good and you make me smile"

"Tasha you've made me a very happy man. I hope you realise that. I know I shouldn't be texting you, I know you have problems at home, but you feel like a part of me and I need to know you are ok!"

"Tasha are you awake?" I hear Mum calling me.

"I'm blushing now and my Mum is calling for me. I'll talk to you later Caleb. Enjoy your day!"

"I'd enjoy it more if I could have coffee with you!"

"Soon, when I'm back at work, I promise :-)"

"I'll hold you to that Tasha ;-)"

I get out of bed, delete his messages, put my phone in my pocket and walk down the stairs.

During breakfast Mum asks if I want to go shopping today, just for a walk and bit of exercise. I say yeah and we get dressed and go off into the City.

We've been in the city for a couple of hours when I need to sit down so I suggest we go for lunch at TGI's, Mum agrees and we walk over to the restaurant. We have to pass the building where I had my interview on Tuesday, where I had a breakdown afterwards. "Mum that's where I went for my interview on Tuesday I'd love to work there."

"Well Tasha you've always gone after what you want and succeeded so I don't see any difference this time" she says looking up and down the building.

As we walk past I see the car that was outside on Tuesday morning when Mr Handsome was staring at me. I wonder if he's in the car? A little shiver goes down my spine as I see the door open and a pair of legs come out of the car.

I can see him side on and I have to stop and just look at him, he's gorgeous. Mum looks at me "Tasha stop staring, then again I can see why you are, he's hot!"

I laugh out loud and he turns towards me at the sound of my laughter. He stops and smiles at me. Once again I find it hard to breathe, it's like time stands still and I've forgotten everything except HIM. I shake my head to get those kind of thoughts out of my head, he then nods his head and walks into the building. I wonder if he is the CEO for the Company I want to work in. Wow! Now that would make every day interesting.

I look at Mum and she's stood there with her mouth open, I put my finger under her chin and close her mouth and I start laughing. I reach out and link arms with her as we walk towards the restaurant. "Did you see the way he looked at you Tasha? I hope he hadn't just had lunch because he looked hungry enough to eat you up. You still got it girl" she says laughing.

When we arrive at the restaurant my phone signals a text. After asking for a table for two I check my phone. It's Caleb!

"I see you are feeling better today Angel. I'm sure I just saw you in town with another gorgeous woman. Hope you're treating yourself, if not then you should. You've had a tough week. Wish I could have stopped to say hello, but I know you're not ready for that."

What!!! He saw me, I can't even remember 100% what he looks like, the memory of him was erased after falling down the stairs. Damn now I'm frustrated.

"Where did you see me?" Maybe I can work this out by process of elimination.

"Ah now that would be telling lol. You'll have to work harder than that to find out"

God he's frustrating, but I like his challenge.

"I know you're that fat, ugly man standing on the corner with the "All you can eat" buffet sign!"

Hope that doesn't piss him off, but he deserves that!

"Ha ha I nearly fell of my chair laughing there Tasha, you are so wrong! Maybe I'm in TGI's looking at you!"

What? He's here? Where? I look around me and there's not a man on his own and no one's texting on their phone. Is he a creep? Spying on me – I need to ask him.

"Should I be freaked that you know where I'm eating lunch? I looked around and there's no one in here that I remember bumping into. Maybe you're just forgettable! ;-)"

"Oh now they're fighting words. I am a little disappointed that you don't remember me I will admit that, but it means I can talk to you and you can get to know ME and not what I look like"

Now I'm intrigued even more. I'm smiling at my phone when Mum clears her throat "Is that Felix, he's certainly put a smile on your face"

I just look at her blankly and then I fire a text off to Felix to tell him where we are if he we wants to meet us. "Yes I was just asking if he wanted to meet us for lunch" my phone beeps again and Felix says he's on his way over. "He's coming now". I feel a bit guilty that she thinks I'm texting Felix, but she wouldn't understand what's happening at the moment. I need someone to talk to that will listen to me moaning and not tell me that I'm imagining it.

Mum smiles, I know she loves Felix and I could never disappoint her and tell her what he has been doing recently, it would break her heart.

I smile back at her and I hear my phone beep. I quickly read my text.

"Tasha?"

"Sorry Caleb I have to go, I like what I've learnt so far, although you sound a bit like a stalker because you keep seeing me and I don't see you - only joking ;-)"

I delete his messages and then turn my phone onto silent so it won't disturb me during lunch.

I see Felix walking into the restaurant as I put my phone back into my pocket. I go to stand to greet him but he holds his hands out to say no. "Hey babe how are you feeling. I was delighted you texted me to meet for lunch. Thanks" he kisses me on the forehead.

"Hi Jean, you managed to drag her out, well done" he sits down next to me and opposite my Mum.

We order lunch and talk about what we bought and what we are doing this afternoon. Me and Mum have decided to go to the cinema to watch a film. It doesn't matter what's on, we just want to see something. Before we know it lunch is over, Felix pays and then goes back to work. Me and Mum link arms and walk down to the Odeon Cinema to see what is showing. They are showing The Internship with Vince Vaughn and Owen Wilson, so we decide to go in and watch it. It was so funny, we laughed all afternoon.

When we get home later that evening, we collapse on the couch because it was such a busy day. We had fun today, it's been a long time since me and Mum did anything like that so I really enjoyed it.

15

FELIX RINGS ME ON his way home to tell me he has a black tie event with work tonight and he wants me to go with him. God I wished he'd said at lunch time, I could have had my hair and make up done while I was out. I know I have to be careful about what I wear because of my bruises. Mum comes upstairs to help me choose a dress, we try a few on, she has to help me because it's a little painful bending and lifting my arms. The one we both like is a bright royal blue with lace insets just above my waist and on the back as a panel. It's gathered slightly on my hips. I love it, it's one of my favourites, I put some black high heeled pumps with it, a plain single diamond necklace and diamond earrings. My Mum helps me to do my long red hair, she puts curls in it and let's it cascade down my back.

I look into the mirror and smile, I look amazing and I feel a million dollars. Mum says "sweetheart you look fabulous, Felix will be so proud" I lose a bit of my smile. I hope he likes it, maybe he won't want me to wear this, he doesn't seem to like me showing myself off recently.

Too late to rethink. I can hear him coming up the stairs. "Tasha, Jean where are you?"

"In here Felix" I shout holding my breath because I hope he likes it and doesn't say anything derogatory in front of Mum.

He opens the door and walks in and stops dead "Wow! Tasha you look beautiful, I'll have to keep my eye on you tonight" he chuckles but I know he doesn't really find it funny.

"Just remember Felix you'll be taking her home tonight not anyone else" she smiles at him and he smiles back.

"I'm very lucky Jean, very lucky! Now both of you out because I need to get changed so we can go." He says indicating the door.

Me and Mum walk out and down the stairs. I take some painkillers because I'm in a little pain with the high heels on, but it should pass.

We stand in the kitchen talking and I remember my phone in my bag. I take it out and am slightly disappointed not to have any new messages from Caleb. I put my phone into my evening bag and don't turn the sound back on.

Felix comes down and we go off to the function, which is in the Bristol Marriott Hotel. It's very upmarket and I can't wait to see inside. We pull up to reception and Felix hands the valet the car keys. Wow this is posh!

We walk into the function room and it's full of people, both men and women. I look around to see if I recognise anyone from work, I can see Peter Frost, our CEO with his wife; Mary Dwyer, our HR Manager and her husband. At least I know some people. As I'm looking around I notice a man staring at me, he's so familiar looking but I can't quite place him. I don't think he works in our company though. I'll have another sneaky look later and see if I can place him.

I hope I don't bump into one of the people who interviewed me, I'd like to think that if I do that they realise I'm here with work and they won't say anything. We walk around and find out where we are sitting for dinner, we are with the others from work and two other couples.

When we sit down to dinner, Felix pulls out the chair for me to sit down, I look up at him and smile, he is being very attentive tonight. We talk to the others around the table as the starter and main course are served. When it comes to dessert I excuse myself from the table and find the ladies room. When I'm in there I take my phone out of my bag to check in with Mum, I didn't really want to leave her at home on her own, but she couldn't come with us. I see I have a text from Caleb waiting for me.

"I thought I saw an Angel tonight wearing a beautiful blue colour?"

What?? Does that mean he is here at the function? Now I'm curious, I want to know what he looks like, or do I? I see the message came through not long after we walked into the function room. I know I will be looking at everyone to see if they are Caleb.

"Now you have intrigued me Caleb. I didn't think I wanted to know what you looked like or who you are, but

knowing you are in the room with me changes everything"

"Really!! I didn't think it would change anything for you. Is that your husband with you? I'm finding it hard not to come over and talk to you and introduce myself. I'd find it harder not to punch him for treating you the way he does"

"How cavalier Caleb!"

"I know, I never experience these feelings and it's very strange Tasha. I would like nothing more than to introduce myself, however, I don't think you really want to yet!"

"True, you know me already! However, I would like a clue, I'm going to be checking all the men out to see if I can work out who you are"

"Oooh now who has fighting talk lol. See you on the dancefloor Tasha"

After deleting my messages, I speak to Mum, she says she is going to go to bed and will make sure I get up to go for my appointment in the morning, then I go back to our table. I find myself looking around the room looking for Caleb, it's quite frustrating that I don't know what he looks like! Then again it is fun!

When I sit down at the table I tell Felix that I have been talking to Mum just in case he wonders why I took so long, he smiles at me and turns to continue talking to Peter.

I eat my dessert and find my eyes still looking around, but no one is looking at me so I can't work it out. After coffee, Felix asks me to dance with him, I say that I will but he has to be careful of my ribs. He smiles and puts out his hand to help pull me up. I wince slightly, my tablets must be wearing off, I'll take some more when I've had a dance.

We go over to the dance floor and Felix pulls me into him and puts his hand onto the lower part of my back and then holds my hand with his other hand. We glide around the dance floor, I'm glad we took lessons to learn to dance properly for our wedding, we work very well together and I concentrate on Felix. He is smiling down at me, when he twirls me around. The pain cuts through me and I make a small scream, Felix pulls me close to him "Don't make a scene Tasha" he whispers in my ear as he continues to dance.

"Felix, that really hurt I need to sit down, I need to take some tablets, please"

"Tasha stop making a scene it was only a small twirl for gods sake" he moans in my ear. I can feel the tears welling in my eyes and I know they are going to overflow onto my face soon if I don't get some control back. I start to pull away from him and he quickly pulls me back." Tasha, I'm warning you, I will drag you away from here kicking and screaming if you fight me" he says.

"Felix please, I'm begging you! I think I'll pass out if I can't sit down and take some tablets" I'm leaning against him and he's moving me around the dance floor. After about 5 minutes which actually seemed like 20 minutes, he stops dancing and pulls me back to the dinner table. I excuse myself to go to the ladies room because I know I need to cry and I don't want to give him the satisfaction of seeing me.

The ladies room is full so I go into the disabled

toilet cubicle and lock the door and sit on the toilet and sob. I take my pain killers, so that they can start kicking in straight away. While I'm sitting on the toilet I start thinking about Felix and why is my life turning into a bad soap opera? I always thought that these kind of things wouldn't happen to me! How did this perfect life turn into a nightmare? When I've stopped sobbing I hear a small knock on the door "Just a minute, I'll be just a minute" I say wiping my face and making sure my make up is straight.

"Tasha is that you in there? Are you ok? I saw what happened, it's me, Caleb" I'd know his voice anywhere after only hearing it a few times.

"Yeah it's me, I'm hurting so bad physically and also emotionally, why me? I've never done anything to hurt anyone ever, I'm not a bad person Caleb"

"I don't know why Tasha, I can't help you with that. Is there anything I can get now to help you. I want to just come in and hug you, but I know that won't make it any better" he's whispering at the door. His voice sounds like melted chocolate and under other circumstances I'm sure I'd be melting too. "I'll wait for you to come out if you want me to, but I think your husband is looking for you. I'm going to go but I will be keeping an eye on you ok!" and with that he leaves.

I feel slightly better that someone else saw what happened and it's not just in my imagination. After a couple of minutes I check myself in the mirror once again and walk out of the toilet. As I'm walking back to the table I see Felix walking towards me. I smile to let him know I'm coming back to the table, but he doesn't look happy. What now?

"We're leaving Tasha, we've been dealing with a client and he just approached Peter and told him that he wasn't going to be dealing with us in future. That's a big contract, which I'd been working on, down the drain, no reason, no nothing. Peter is not a happy man! So we are going home. You can drive, I've had a drink!" he is furious.

He pulls me into the lift after him and he can't even look at me." I didn't get chance to say goodbye Felix" I say.

"Don't worry they were too engrossed in a conversation with Mr Hunt to be bothered whether you said goodbye or not" he sneers at me. I decide at this point to just go along with anything he says. We walk through reception and out to the valet, who collects our car when we hand in the ticket. We get into the car and I drive home in silence, it was such a lovely evening and then it was spoilt for two reasons, one Felix and two his client. It really hurts for me to drive the car, because I have to keep twisting to see behind me.

When we get back to the house, I remind Felix that Mum is asleep in the house and we go off to bed. I hope he doesn't touch me tonight, I don't think I can take his anger tonight! I have to ask him to undo my zip so that I can step out of my dress. I have lacey matching underwear underneath and I hope he doesn't get turned on when he sees it. Thankfully, he seems to be in such a bad mood he doesn't even notice. I put my nightdress on and climb into bed and lie facing the wall and I can feel myself drifting off to sleep when I feel the bed move as Felix gets into it. I can feel myself holding my breath in case he moves onto my side of the bed, he doesn't

"Goodnight Tasha, you looked beautiful tonight, I'm sorry" and then he goes silent. There are silent tears running down my cheeks, I didn't think I had any tears left.

16

AGAIN, I WAKE AFTER Felix has gone to work, my head is hurting from all the crying. I don't know what to do! I don't understand what is happening with my marriage, I don't know whether to say something to Mum or not. I'm really torn because I talk to Mum about everything and I never hide anything from her, but I just don't think she would believe me. That would hurt the most, if she didn't believe me! She'd probably think I was being a drama queen or something. So I decide not to say anything!

I check my phone and see a few texts from Caleb and one from Felix. I read Felix's text first.

"Babe I'm sorry about last night, I was being totally selfish and you looked so beautiful, I'm sorry"

I don't know how I feel about that. I don't want to think about Felix right now, I'm so confused. I read Caleb's texts.

"Tasha are you ok? You didn't return after I spoke to you; please let me know you are ok!"

"My Angel please let me know you are ok, I won't sleep until I hear from you"

Surely he knew I wouldn't be able to text him last night, it was far too intense between me and Felix.

"Tasha, please!" That last one was sent at 5am this morning.

"Caleb I hope you did go to sleep, I wasn't able to send a message last night, things were a little intense. When I came out of the toilet he was looking for me because a client had told them they were not going to work with them again"

"Oh my god Tasha you don't know how happy I am to hear from you. I was so worried about you and I had no other way of getting hold of you. I'm so glad you are ok. You are Ok aren't you?"

"Yes I am ok Caleb, honestly. I was in pain last night but I'm ok now after a good nights sleep. Can I ask you something?"

"You can ask me anything Tasha, I'll always be honest with you ;-)"

"Were you the Client?"

"Yes I was, I hope that didn't cause you anymore trouble but I couldn't work with someone who treats a person the way you were treated. Yes, it did make a difference that it was you, but I would have done it to anyone. Are you mad with me?"

"No, I know you were looking out for me and I

appreciate it. Thanks Caleb"

"Anything for you Tasha! I have a meeting now so I'll catch up with you later.I know you have your check up later today, please let me know how you get on, my interest in coffee is depending on it ☺"

"I'm sure you're a stalker ☺"

"Ha ha good luck"

I can hear Mum moving around, so I carefully climb out of bed and go down stairs. Mum asks questions about last night while she is making coffee and breakfast. I'm tempted to say something, but I know she won't believe me.

Soon its time to go to the hospital, Mum drives us in my car and then we go and wait in the clinic. Mum insists on coming into the check up with me, the doctor asks me to remove my top so that he can examine my bruising. I do as he says and just stare at the wall. It's the same doctor that I had when I stayed overnight, I can feel that he wants to say something to me but doesn't because Mum is there. Good I don't feel like talking anyway. After he finishes the examination he tells me to get dressed, he says that I can go back to work but that my ribs would be painful for another few weeks. He bandaged the ribs up and showed me how to ensure that the bandages were tight enough to keep the ribs from hurting.

I have to go back in two weeks for an xray and another check up, but I'm just happy that I can go back to work. The doctor asks to see me for a few minutes on my own, Mum says she will wait outside for me.

"So Natasha, how are you managing? Have you

found it hard to do things?" he asks.

"Some things have been a bit difficult but I've had help. I went to a work function last night and when I was dancing I pulled my ribs a little, the pain was quite bad, but I had my pain killers to hand."

"Hmm you don't want to be taking the pain killers for a long time either, I want you to reduce the amount of times you take them in a day, if you can and see how you get on. How's the situation at home? Any better?"

"I'm not sure I know what you mean doctor" I'm being coy because I'm not ready to talk about it.

"Ok Natasha, do you still have the numbers I gave you?" he asks. I nod "Good, now I'll see you in two weeks ok"

I stand and shake his hand "Thank you doctor, I appreciate all the help you've given me" I turn and walk out the door to my Mum.

We get in the car and then head towards home. "So Tasha I suppose that means I can go home today, I get the feeling though that I'm still needed, what do you want me to do?" she looks at me, she's very intuitive.

"I'd like you to stay tonight and then we can go home and see Dad and have lunch together. All of us" I don't want her to go yet. I need my Mum.

"That sounds like a good idea sweetheart, I'll ring your Dad when we get to yours and make sure he buys in stuff for lunch" she's smiling so I know she's happy.

We have lunch when we get home and Kammie rings to say she is on her way over. She didn't make it the other day when we went shopping. I hope she has some gossip for us, I can't wait. It will take the spotlight off me.

I ring Felix to tell him how the check up went and to tell him Mum is staying the night and then we will have lunch when we take her home. He seems to be ok with that, we talk about the weekend and what we will do with the rest of the time.

Then, I text Caleb to let him know that I'm ok and going back to work.

"Hey just letting you know that I'm going back to work on Monday. I'm bandaged up but able to move around ;-)"

"That's great news! Maybe we will get coffee one day. How are you after last night? How's the pain?"

"The pain isn't too bad, I just needed the pain killers last night and I slept well. My friend is on her way over to have a gossip and a laugh, so that is great therapy in it's self"

"Just don't laugh too hard it might hurt! I'm glad you can go back to work on Monday Tasha, really I am"

"Thanks Caleb me too. She's here now so I have to go. Talk to you later??"

"I'd talk to you all day if I could Tasha. Talk later x"

Did he just put a kiss at the end of his text? I hope he's not reading too much into this. Am I leading him astray? Should I stop texting him? It's good to talk to someone who is impartial to Felix, although I'm sure Caleb is slightly biased. I need to think about what I'm doing with Caleb, I'll think about it later!

Kammie walks into the kitchen and sits herself down, "Any tea going?"

"Make yourself at home Kammie" I laugh. She chuckles too and Mum stands up and pours her a cup of tea.

When Mum sits down she looks at Kammie and says "Sooooo, any news or gossip Kammie?" typical Mum to get straight to the point.

"Well I met Luca the other day for a drink and we talked about a lot of things, we also talked about you and Felix telling us that we couldn't' take our relationship any further because it could have implications down the line if we didn't work out. I like him though and I know he likes me. I sometimes wonder whether we would be able to make it work or not." She sighs as she obviously isn't happy.

"Ah Kammie that is bullshit, if two people like each other then they should be together, nevermind what will happen in the future. We are all adults and can deal with break ups and friends hanging together, I think you two should be together, you are both amazing people and just imagine what you could have, don't mind what me and Felix said all that time ago, we didn't have the right to keep you and Luca apart" I say as I've grabbed her hand and started rubbing it.

"Yeah Kammie I have to agree with Tasha on this one, you both need to stop being scared of any kind of commitment and take one day at a time. You would make a perfect couple, just like Felix and Tasha" I take my hand away from Kammie and look at the floor, I can't look at either of them.

"Yes Kammie, you would make the perfect couple" I stand up and make my way over to the coffee machine to pour another coffee just so that I can avoid her eyes, which I know are searching and understanding there is a problem with Mr and Mrs Perfect. Kammie knows me too well to not see that there is something wrong. I look at her then and hope she knows not to say anything in front of Mum.

"Well we did have a good night the other night and I did get a goodnight kiss that absolutely blew my socks off" she laughs.

"Ah! So there is more to this story!" Mum says. "You know if it's meant to be then it will happen. Fate is something you can't avoid. I believe full heartedly in fate, you know that Tasha don't you"

I nod, that's twice I've heard about fate this week. "Yeah you certainly do Mum" I smile at her. I know she met Dad when she bumped into him on the street and his papers blew away. That was fate intervening! Maybe there's more to this fate thing than I think.

We sit and gossip for another couple of hours and then Kammie has to go, I walk her to the door and she takes me into a hug and says "You look very unhappy Tasha and I know there's something wrong with you. Luca told me to keep a close eye on you, that he was worried about you since the accident. I can see what he means! We need a night out or a night in together just us girls. Let me know when suits" she kisses me on the cheek and then disappears out to her car.

"Yeah Kammie I'll arrange something" I shout after her retreating body.

I close the door and walk back to Mum, who is preparing dinner for us all.

I hear my phone beep and check my messages.

"Hi Tasha, how are you now?"

"Hi Caleb, I'm good, my friend just left so I've had a great afternoon"

"Good you need some time to make you smile. You looked so unhappy last night and I just wanted to sweep you up and take you away x"

"Thanks but I'm not that light LOL"

"I'm sure I could lift you easily my Angel"

"Hmm we'll see about that ;-)"

"I'd definitely like to try!"

"Ok this is not where I envisaged this conversation going. I hope I'm not encouraging you too much. You know my situation!"

"Tasha, unfortunately I DO know your situation and I don't like it but I want to be your friend. Yes, I think you are the most beautiful creature who ever walked or fell into my life, but more than that I want to be your friend"

"Wow, that's good because I want you to be my friend too. I love getting your messages and being able to tell you anything. Caleb, I want to thank you for helping me through to this terrible week ;-)"

"Anytime Tasha anytime. I hope you don't have anymore weeks like this one but I'm here if you ever need anything ok?"

"Thanks Caleb, thanks so much. You make me want to cry you are so nice to me"

"I'd like to be nicer to you ;-) but I know that's not where you want to go. I'll settle on just knowing you!"

I don't reply to that because I'm not 100% sure that I don't want it to go that way and I'm married and I shouldn't be thinking like that.

My phone rings and I look at the number, it's a number I don't recognise. I answer the phone and it's Helen about the Administration Manager's job with Blue Eye.

"We were really impressed with your attitude to work particularly under the circumstances and we would like to invite you in to meet our CEO Mr Hunt on Friday at 8.00am" she says.

I need to take a breath. This is the job I really want and they want me to meet their CEO wow! "That's great news, yes of course I'll be able to meet Mr Hunt, I'd be delighted. Thank you"

I hang up the phone and then tell Mum, she is delighted for me, I can't wait to tell Felix, so I ring him, he seems excited for me "That's great Tasha, is that the one you had on Monday?" he asks.

"No it's the one I had on Tuesday Felix, I haven't heard from the first one, maybe I won't get any further with that interview" I say.

"I'm not sure that's the best job for you to take Tasha, you're good with facilities and that's what the first job is about. You've never worked in marketing before" now he doesn't sound happy at all.

"Felix that's why it would be good to do this, it would be challenging and I'm ready for a challenge" I say back to him.

"We will talk about it over the weekend Tasha" and with that he dismisses me and hangs up.

What now? He doesn't seem to ever be happy with me these days. Something to look forward to I suppose, an exciting discussion over the weekend. I can't help but be sarcastic because I just can't do anything right!

Just before Felix is due home, I receive another call, this time from Debbie in HR at the Clifton Associates "Hi Natasha, hope you are well, we were very interested in you after your interview with Mr Wolfe and would like to invite you to a further interview with the CEO on Wednesday at 8.00am. Is that suitable?"

Wow another interview, this day is just getting better "Thank you I'd love to come along on Wednesday, thanks"

We finalise the plans and then I hang up.

"Mum you are never going to believe this, but that was the other company and they were inviting me to another interview too." I'm really happy and feel like things are coming together for me.

We talk about the two jobs and I tell her I prefer the one on Friday, but that I would actually take either one. I get excited about it and can feel the adrenalin buzzing through me.

The night flows along very nicely with the three of us talking about the two jobs and which one would be better for me.

17

BEFORE I KNOW IT it's Saturday and time to take Mum home.

When we get to Mum's, Dad has lunch ready so we go straight into the dining room.

Lunch was lovely and I spend the time telling Dad about the two interviews that I have lined up.

When we leave Mum and Dad's, Felix takes my hand and holds it while he is driving. "I can't wait to have you to myself so that I can look after you" he says. I just look at him and smile. I don't trust myself to say anything.

On the way home my phone beeps with a text so I take it out to read it. I see it is from Caleb and I can feel my heart racing because I know if Felix saw it he would be angry! I know I need to stop texting Caleb, I just can't!

"Hey Tasha hope you are having a good weekend. I was just thinking about you and thought I'd let you

know"

I turn the ringer off and put it in my pocket without replying, I'll do that later. Felix asks "Who was that?"

"It was Kammie she wants to know if I can go over for a girls night next week, we haven't done that since I got married" how easy a lie came, what am I doing? My heart is in my mouth, I'm sure Felix can hear it beating really heavy.

"I don't want you to go! I want you to stay with me all the time, I need you, you're my wife" Did he just say that? I can't keep quiet and he's driving so he can't get too mad.

"Felix when you married me I had friends. I still need my friends and I want to go and see her. You didn't mind before we were married what's the difference now?" I'm fuming.

"I didn't like it then but I put up with it because I love you and wanted you to be my wife. Now you are, you only need me, no one else!" he is shouting really loud and I can see he is going red in the face. I also notice that we are pulling up to the house. He stops the car, almost abandoning it in the drive, and gets out, he comes over to my side and opens my door, he reaches in and pulls me out, twisting my ribs at the same time.

"Ow Felix you're hurting me. Stop! Please!" I shout at him, I hope the neighbours aren't watching

"No Tasha, you don't get to talk to me like that and get away with it, I am your HUSBAND and I demand respect! You will do what I say and go where I tell you you can go and I'm telling you I don't want you to go over to Kammie's house, not this week, not next week, not ever. She is a bad influence on you and I want her out of your life" what the heck? Where has this man come from? Where is the Felix I knew?

He opens the front door and turns around and locks it, then he pulls me to stand facing him and then all of a sudden he punches me in the face. I feel the pain and I stumble backwards and then fall to the floor sobbing hysterically "Felix what has got into you recently? You were never like this, what happened to you?"

"You! You happened to me, you came into my life and turned it upside down. I want you so much, I have you forever and I don't want to share you with anyone including your family and friends. Tasha I can't share you!" he is leaning over me and I can see he's crying. My life is so surreal right now. What is going on with him? Why does he feel like he can't share me? I just don't understand what is going on in his mind!

"Felix you have me and you don't have to share me but you need to understand that I will need other people in my life. You're the one who takes me home and keeps me" I'm pleading with him, the pain of my cheek is horrendous, I think he must have broken a bone and I can feel the hot sticky blood running down my face and mixing in with my tears. I now realise that after today that I need to talk to someone, I need to talk to my Mum! She is the only one who can help me now, she has to believe me. She needs to believe me!

"No Tasha YOU don't understand! You are not going to leave this house unless it's with me or going to work. I can't run around wondering where you are? Who you're with? And what you're saying to them. I know you'll tell Kammie that I'm not who you thought I was. I just know it!!" and with that he grabs me and pulls my hair so that I'm standing and he pushes me against the wall and attacks my mouth with his. He forces his tongue inside and all I want to do is bite it to get it out of my mouth. I turn my head to try and get away, he doesn't like that so he puts his two hands on either side of my head and holds it in place.

This is obviously turning him on because I can feel his cock through his jeans rubbing against me. He moves one of his hand down to undo my jeans and I struggle even more, he can't do his and get away with it surely? He pulls my jeans and panties down and then unbuckles his belt, he quickly pushes his jeans and boxers down and then pushes me up to the wall, he takes both of my hands in one of his and then he holds them above my head, tightly. He takes the other hand and takes his cock in it firmly as he's trying to find my pussy. I'm dry because I'm not turned on and he forces himself inside, because I'm dry it hurts and I scream "STOP" but he doesn't listen to me. I decide there and then not to fight him, there isn't any point, it will only make it worse. So I just give up and let him finish what he started. He just keeps pounding into me, groaning "Tasha that feels so good, you're so tight, you're mine, mine, mine!" and then I feel him cum. Thank god it's over, I have tears dripping off my chin. I need to talk to my Mum. Felix might let me go to bed now that he has assaulted me, I really need to get away from him and ring my Mum.

He leans against me not releasing my hands "See how good we are Tasha, we fit together perfectly" I don't know what planet he just stepped off but he needs to go back there because none of that was good for me.

"Answer me Tasha, tell me it was good! TELL ME!" he shouts in my ear.

I start squirming and don't say anything, he brings one hand down and takes my chin between his fingers and says "SAY IT TASHA"

I shake my head because I can't say it. Before I know it he's pushed my head against the wall with a thump and then he twirls me so that I'm in front of him with my hands behind my back. He marches me over to the couch and roughly pushes me over the top of it, my bare ass in the air. What is he going to do to me now?

"Say it Tasha say we are good together" he's so angry he's spitting on me, at this stage I just want him to kill me so that I don't have to go through this again, no such luck. He smacks me on the ass and I scream, he does it again. "Do you know how many times I've wanted to smack your ass, do you?" he keeps doing it and then he starts to play with my ass, slowly spreading my cheeks and then running his finger around the rim. "Even this is mine Tasha every single millimetre of you is mine" with that he pushes his finger inside and I cry out, but I don't give him the satisfaction of knowing how much it hurts me.

He's moving his finger in and out at a quick pace and then he takes his finger out, he bends down and licks the rim with his tongue and pushes his tongue inside a small way. When he pulls his tongue out he spits on my ass and then starts rubbing it onto my rim. I don't know what he's doing but he's grunting while he does it. Just as I think things can't get any worse he takes hold of his cock and pushes it into my ass. The pain is unbearable and I can't help myself except to scream. I scream so

135

loud he says "Shut up Tasha or do you want me to fuck your mouth to shut you up" I know he would too. So I stop screaming and just sob silently.

When he finally cums he says "Now every part of you belongs to me Tasha I love you" I can't say it back, I just can't.

When he pulls out, he falls on top of me and I flinch and try to pull away. "Have you not realised that you need to do what I say and not fight me Tasha. It will make life much easier"

He stands up and pulls his jeans up and then he pulls up my panties and jeans too. He then slaps my ass and walks away. I run upstairs into the bathroom and lock the door and I roll into a ball sobbing. After about 15 minutes, I start running a bath, then I turn and look in the mirror. My cheek has a huge bruise on it and its swollen and starting to throb, I look through the bathroom cabinet to see if I have any painkillers there, no such luck they are on my bedside table. Will I leave the sanctity of the bathroom or will I stay here. I opt to stay, give Felix chance to calm down, if that is ever going to happen.

Finally, the bath is run and I take my clothes off and step into the bath, I don't care that it is boiling and my skin is turning bright red. I lay down in the water and slowly sink under it and hold my breath for as long as I can and then I jump up gasping for breath. I lay back down and start to scrub my skin with the loofah we have laid on the side of the bath, my skin is on fire, it starts to bleed but I really don't care. After I have scrubbed myself and I feel satisfied that I'm not dirty any longer I lay back down and cry.

I must have fallen asleep because when I jolt back up the water is cold, I don't want to get out but my body is starting to look like a prune, all wrinkled and cold.

Once I've dried myself off. I wrap myself in my dressing gown which is hanging on the back of the door, I pick up my clothes and I walk across to my bedroom and put my pyjamas on. I open the drawer and take out the pain killers and my sleeping tablets, I have a glass of water from last night, but I don't care and swallow them.

I contemplate taking all of the sleeping tablets at once, just so that I don't have to deal with Felix again. I know that isn't the solution but right now I don't know what the solution is! I remember my clothes so I go over to them and throw them into the bin, I never want to wear them again. Before I put them in the bin I remember my phone in my pocket, what good is it anyway? No one would believe me if I told them. I check my phone and see another text from Caleb, god I don't need this right now!

"Are you ok?"

I turn the phone off because I don't want to deal with this anymore. I can't deal with this anymore. I thought maybe by me telling Caleb it would make it better for me, but even if I tell him, what can he do? Nothing! He can't do anything to make it better for me! Not even Mum can make it better, I'm not sure I can tell her, I know I should, but she doesn't really need to know. Felix will get better, I'm certain he will. I know that I just need to deal with it myself, I'm strong, I can get through this! I climb into bed and curl into a ball and hope the drugs take effect soon because I don't want to remember any of this. I can feel myself getting tired and I allow the darkness to swallow me up and I hope that I never wake up!

18

ALL OF A SUDDEN I hear someone screaming and I jump up with a start, I look around the room, and then I realise it's me screaming.

My heart is racing and I'm sweating! I look over and Felix is staring at me. "Oh my god Tasha, are you ok? You don't look great, what can I get you? Do you need any medication? Are you going to be ok?" he reaches out to push my hair off my face and I jump out of bed screaming.

"No, no, no get off me, leave me alone Felix, please don't touch me" I curl into a ball in the corner of the bedroom. I can feel my heart racing so fast and I'm sweating, all I feel is fear!

Felix gets out of the bed and comes over to me, he kneels down in front me, making sure he doesn't touch me and then he starts crying " Tasha I'm sorry, I just feel that I'm going to lose you now that I have you and I can't live without you. I don't know what I would do without you, you are my life, my love, my heart" .He looks at me, but I really don't know what to say. For the first time, I feel nothing when I look at him!

I know it's the middle of the night so I stand up carefully, making sure I don't touch Felix and I walk over to my bedside table and take another sleeping tablet, just to help get me through the rest of the night. I then walk out of the bedroom and into the spare room and climb into bed. I've never slept in the spare room before, I've always slept with Felix, but tonight I don't want to be anywhere near him. I'm asleep almost instantly and I don't wake up until 11am on Sunday morning.

When I wake up, the first thing I notice is that it is so quiet, not a radio nor a TV is on, so I get out of the bed and walk out of the room. I walk to my bedroom and open the door, the room is empty, but all my perfumes and ornaments are broken into small pieces on the floor, the lights are smashed and I can see blood on the mirror and it is shattered. What happened in here after I left last night? I don't know if I want to know or not! Where is Felix? What did he do? I start to get worried about him, I hope he's ok! I don't want to be near him, but I don't want him to be hurt either. I walk over to my bedside table and take out my pain killers, my face is screaming in agony. I take two of them and take my phone out of the drawer, then I turn and walk down the stairs to see if everything is ok downstairs.

Everything seems to be ok and I walk into the kitchen and see Felix asleep with his head on the kitchen table. I walk past him trying not to wake him, but as I go to move past him, his hand flies off the table and catches my arm. I flinch and start to pull backwards, but he pulls me closer to the table, I start to cry "Felix no please don't, I'm in so much pain, please. I can't take any more!"

He slowly lifts his head and lets go of my arm, "I only wanted to see how you were this morning, did you manage to get any sleep? How is your cheek? I see you cleaned it up. You'll be able to hide that with make up, it's only a bit swollen" he tries to reach out and touch my cheek, but I turn my face. I don't want him to touch me, especially where it hurts so much after what he did to me!

I walk past him and put the coffee machine on, I'm in dire need of a shot of caffeine, the sleeping tablets always make me drowsy in the mornings, particularly seeing as I took some in the middle of the night too." Do you really want me to answer those questions Felix? I don't think I can! What happened in the bedroom?"

"I was so angry with myself when you went into the other bedroom. We've never slept in separate beds since we got together and I never wanted that to happen to us. I guess I got angry and took it out on the bedroom. I'm sorry Tasha, I love you" he says with remorse. I can't believe he's really sorry, he's just saying it.

"Felix what have I done to make you act like this? It's just so not like you. You're going to push me away if you keep doing this" I can't look at him, I don't want to look at him right now.

"I'm going to have my cup of coffee, then I'm going to tidy myself up and I'm going for a walk, I expect you to clean up that mess upstairs because I can't bear to look at you or the mess right now" I turn towards the coffee machine and pour myself a coffee and then go back upstairs before Felix can say anything. I get dressed and put a little bit of make up on to cover my bruise, then I go back down the stairs and out of the front door. I slam it shut! I walk down the street and across the road to the park, I sit down on the swings and I just shut off. I don't think about anything because I don't know what to think. Why is he behaving like this? What did I do to him to make him want to hurt me? I know that he would do anything to protect me and keep me safe and yet he is the one I need saving from.

I think I must have sat there for an hour and then I remember my phone in my pocket. I look at it and see numerous missed calls from Felix and a couple of voicemails. I ignore them, I have a text from Kammie telling me that she and Luca went out the previous night and had a good time. I'm delighted for her and send her a quick text to let her know that I'm happy for her, I don't tell her anything about Felix, she doesn't need to know.

"So when are you coming over for a girls night Tasha?"

"Not this week Kammie, I have my two interviews. Maybe next week ok?"

"Yeah that's fine, just don't be a stranger. Love you"

"I won't. Love you too"

I'm sad because I want to talk to Kammie, but I don't really want anyone else to know what is happening in my marriage, everything would turn nasty if I tell someone who is so close to me and then I would have to deal with the issue and I'm not sure I have the strength for that right now. I decide to walk for a bit and see where it takes me. I hear my phone beep again and take it out to look at it. It's Caleb.

"Tasha are you ok? Please answer me, I'm getting worried, I can't think about anything else, please!"

I want to answer him, I really do, but I don't think it's the right thing to do after what happened last night.

Then again, I can't help myself, he is someone who wants to make sure I'm ok, wants to look after me and right now I need looking after. I know it is the wrong thing to do, but I also know that I need someone to lean on too and Felix isn't that person right now.

"Caleb, I'm sorry, things have been a bit mad around here. Thank you for worrying about me"

"Tasha of course I worry about you. Since you stumbled into my life, I can't think of anything else. Tell me honestly, are you ok?"

"No, no I'm not"

"Where are you? I'll come and get you"

"No you can't do that, it will make things worse, please Caleb just talk to me, it will help to make me feel better"

My phone rings and I hesitate to answer it.

"Where are you, please let me help you Tasha!" Caleb says, and I can hear the worry in his voice.

"No Caleb, I can't, but I like knowing that you are worrying about me. We will get coffee soon, but right now I have a lot going on."

"Tasha, this is not about the coffee, this is about me wanting to help you, needing to know that you are ok. Remember I told you about fate, well I truly believe that we will meet soon. I'm here if you ever need rescuing ok?"

"Thanks Caleb, I know you are, talk soon ok, I'll make sure to let you know I'm fine, then you won't need to worry about me"

"I don't think you really understand me Tasha, I will always worry about you, especially while you are in that house with that man. If I can't drag you away from the house then I will keep checking on you and you need to get used to it."

"I know Caleb and I can't explain to you how much that means to me. Thank you from the bottom of my heart, you are here for me when no one else is and I know that is my doing because I haven't spoken to anyone about it, but I know you will listen to me"

"I will always be available to listen to you Tasha, remember you fell into my life for a reason. Now send me a message later to let me know you are home and you are fine, please Tasha" he hangs up.

I'm so confused, my life is taking a turn which I never expected and I don't really know how to handle it.

My phone beeps with a message from Felix

"Please come home Tasha, I love you and I'm sorry, I'll look after you I promise"

I start sobbing and decide that I have to go home and see Felix, I need him to tell me that everything is going to be ok. I need Felix to start treating me right, to show me he loves me because right now I think he hates me!

I walk slowly towards home and then as I go to open the door, Felix opens it from the inside, he pulls me into a hug and I can see he has been crying. "Babe I thought you weren't coming back and you had left me. I even rang Kammie to see if you were there, she said she had heard from you and that you sounded fine, she said she would text if she heard from you again."

"Felix why did you ring her, surely you knew I would come back. We need to work on some things, but I wouldn't leave you" I can't believe I said that, but I guess I must really mean it. I married this man because I loved him and wanted to spend the rest of my life with him, I'm not going to give up on that just because of a few mishaps, we can talk about this and sort it out. Right?

We spend the rest of the day talking and crying and by the end of the night Felix has agreed that he will go to see a doctor, it appears he is having anxiety attacks because he thinks I'll leave him, although I've given him no cause to think that. He apologised time and time again that he wasn't himself at the moment and that he loves me, I believe him because I love him and I know he's not himself.

When we go to bed, Felix cuddles into me but doesn't try anything sexual thankfully, I'm not sure I'm ready for that yet. After last night, it will take a while for me to be ready to have sex with Felix, I don't really want him to touch me, but he hugs me and doesn't move his hands up and down my body, they stay in one place all night.

The next few days go along as normal, I manage to hide my injuries with a good bit of make up, so no one at work can see the bruises. After dinner on Tuesday night, we sit and start talking about my two interviews and realise that the first one is tomorrow morning, this is the one that Felix wants me to take; I'd prefer the other one, but I don't tell him that.

Wednesday morning comes and once again, Felix has put out my clothes for my interview, another trouser suit and a high neck blouse. I thought we had been getting somewhere with his trust issues, but obviously not.

Felix drops me to the interview himself and wishes me luck. When it is over he is there waiting to collect me and take me to work.

It's like he doesn't trust me or something. He wants to know where I am at all times. I'm happy to go along with it as long as angry Felix stays away. I don't miss him!

19

FRIDAY MORNING COMES around quickly and I get up feeling great about my interview. As seems to be the norm these days Felix has put my clothes out for me, it's easier not to say anything and just wear what he puts out. I put my make up on, making sure I put extra on my cheek because my bruise is very yellow, the swelling has nearly all gone but you can see the bruise without any make up on.

I drive myself into the city today as Felix has a meeting across town, I park near the Blue Eye Building. I walk into the building and make my presence known to the receptionist, the last time I was here I saw her name badge said Megan, she is really chatty, I really like her. Megan tells me to sit and wait until Helen, the HR lady will come and get me. I feel a bit anxious today and I'm not sure why, maybe it's because I really want this job.

Helen comes and takes me to a meeting room, all the walls are glass and I can see everyone looking at me. She tells me that we can see out but because she turned a knob on the glass, no one can see in. "Take a seat

Natasha, Mr Hunt will be here in a few minutes. He has asked that I introduce him then leave you alone for him to conduct the interview and then he will call me in for the remainder of the interview" she says smiling at me.

I've never had an interview like that before, but there's a first time for everything I suppose. I take a seàt at the table, I can see a man walking towards the door, he stops just outside and then he takes a deep breath and opens the door. My heart is already racing, this man looks familiar, he's the man with the car, he's the man who was staring at me, he's Mr Handsome. But it's more than that and I can't quite put my finger on it, I've seen him somewhere else, I just can't remember where.

The door opens and Helen stands up and in walks Mr Handsome, wow he really is gorgeous. "Natasham this is Mr Hunt" Helen says. I hold out my hand for him to shake it.

He takes my hand and smiles at me "Pleased to meet you Natasha."

Helen walks to the door "Natasha, Mr Hunt will conduct the interview and I'll be back in a short while" and she walks out the door and closes it behind her.

Mr Hunt is looking at me like he is trying to figure something out, I don't know whether he is waiting for me to say something or not. So I just sit there looking at him. I smile but I feel awkward, he walks over to the window looking at me but not saying a word, this is the strangest interview I've ever been in. I'm not sure I'm comfortable being scrutinized like this.

Mr Hunt clears his throat, he's moved to stand behind me so I can't see him "Tasha how are you today?"

It seems like the world slows down and stops, it

feels like I can't breathe. "Caleb is that you?" I can't turn around, I'm rooted to the spot, I hold my breath. No way, this can't be right! He knew all along that we would meet today, why didn't he say something so that I could be prepared?

I can feel him coming up behind me, every nerve ending is standing to attention. "Don't turn around, please! I want to explain myself before I see your face. When you bumped into me and then gave me your number I wasn't going to ring you because of the way you left Jesters on that Saturday night. I didn't want to give you anymore trouble, but I couldn't stop thinking about you. I couldn't believe my luck when I saw you on the Monday morning sitting in my reception. I rang you from the car outside and I was watching you the whole time. When I saw you sitting there, time just stood still and I walked back to reception to check that it was you. I wanted to approach you, wanted to see how you were after Saturday night, but behind your beauty I could see your pain." I can feel him stood right behind me and he lifts his hand and slowly puts it on my shoulder. I flinch slightly because he touched me and I didn't realize he was going to touch me.

"I'm sorry Tasha" he says removing his hand. "I have been so worried about you this week, you haven't answered my calls or replied to my texts. Are you ok? Are you angry with me?"

Am I? I don't know what I am right now apart from being confused.

"Caleb I'm really angry, all this time you knew I was trying to get a job here. You never said once, not once that you knew I was coming to this interview. Am I only here because you want to come clean? How can you do this to me? Have I just been a pawn in a game you are playing to amuse yourself?" I'm stood up at this stage and walking towards the door, I still haven't turned around, I don't know if I want to look at him. I am so mad right now!

Just as I reach the door Caleb reaches for the handle and slowly prises my hand off the handle. I can feel the electricity shooting up my arm "Tasha don't go, please. I knew you were going to be angry, I was going to tell you this week but I couldn't reach you, so I didn't get a chance. I know that's not an excuse. Yes, I knew you were being interviewed for the Administration Manager's job. Yes. I kept an eye on your progress but I had nothing to do with you getting this far. You did that all by yourself, I will not influence their decision. Please Tasha look at me, I'm sorry that I lied to you"

I gulp my breath and then slowly turn around, he still has hold of my hand. When I've turned around I am looking at the most magnificent man in the world, he looks sad and scared and then his eyes land on my cheek, his free hand comes up and caresses it very gently, I flinch but I don't move "What happened Tasha?" He's barely controlling his anger.

"I, I, fell Caleb not that it's any of your business. I think I'm going to go, I can't work here after you pulling business from Felix at the ball the other night. There is no way he will let me work for you. After our friendship it doesn't feel right because I wouldn't know if I achieved the position on my own or not and I can't work like that" I say and I can feel a lone tear starting to roll down my cheek.

"Tasha stop! Firstly our friendship has nothing to do with you being here, yes I admit I wanted to meet you today, but you're here because you deserve to be here. Secondly, what difference does it make if Felix doesn't want you to work here, it's your life. Thirdly, I don't believe you fell. Talk to me Tasha you could do it before this week, what happened to change that?" He's still caressing my cheek and I can feel myself leaning into his hand, I just can't help myself. He makes me feel safe.

"Caleb I told you I fell! I have to get out of here, I'm confused, I really wanted this job and now I know I can't take it even if I get offered it. This was supposed to be a great day and now it's turned into the worst day ever. I'm really mad with you, I don't want to see you or talk to you right now Caleb. I'm leaving, tell Helen I said goodbye!" I can't believe this has happened, I really wanted this job.

Before I can react, Caleb leans down and kisses me and I can feel it is a kiss from his heart, it has so much meaning and I end up kissing him back. All of a sudden I realise what is happening and I pull back. "Caleb what the hell did you do that for?" I slap him on the face.

"I'm sorry Tasha, I had to kiss you, I know you're mad with me for many reasons, but I had to taste your lips at least once, I'm sorry" he says as he reaches past me and opens the door. As I walk past him, he whispers in my ear "Just for the record Tasha that was the most amazing two minutes of my life and I'm not giving up on you" he stands up and says in a loud voice "Thanks Natasha for coming in today, we will let you know in the next few days" and then he closes the door behind me, leaving me standing outside the door. A few people turned to look at the door closing, so I walk slowly and calmly out of the room and out to reception. I walk out of the building and walk straight to the nearest coffee shop, I really need a caffeine injection right now. When I've sat at the table, I start to cry, like really hard sobbing. What has happened to my perfect life? I thought that I would get married and live happily ever after. Felix was my happy ever after, I'm not sure I believe that now. How could I have kissed Caleb, I'm married for gods sake. I bury my head in my hands and sob until I feel a hand on my shoulder. I jump in my seat and let out a small yelp!

"Tasha, I'm sorry I had to make sure you were ok, please talk to me, I need to know you are ok"

"Caleb please, I don't know what is happening to me, when you kissed me I should have pulled away straight away, I'm married, I shouldn't be kissing other men. What if Felix finds out? What am I going to say? What will he do to me?" I start sobbing really loud now.

"I'm really sorry, I couldn't help myself, I know I was being selfish, but I really did need to taste you at least once in my lifetime! I can't explain how I feel about you, you wouldn't understand. I know I scare you and I don't mean too, but I need you in my life, please talk to me" I can see he is struggling really hard not to reach out and hug me.

"Ok, sit down, but I need to talk first ok!" I say looking him right in the eyes.

"OK I'll go and get a coffee first, do you want a top up?" I nod and he walks off to the counter. I shake my head, because I don't know what I'm doing, but I also know that Caleb means something to me and I don't want to push him away. I also know that I need to go to work, so I ring in and explain that I was called away to a meeting on my way to work and that I would be there in about an hour. Putting a time limit on this conversation makes me feel better.

Caleb brings my coffee over and sits down "OK I'm all ears" he says, sipping his coffee.

I can't help but look as his lips touch his cup and how he moves them when he takes a sip of the very hot coffee, I can only imagine what his lips could do to me. Where did that come from? I shake my head to get rid of those thoughts, they won't do me any good thinking about him like that.

"Ok, I've worked really hard to get where I am at work. I wanted to look for another job for a challenge, to make work more enjoyable than it is. I need something to sink my teeth into" I see him start to smile and I just look at him and he stops smiling and drinks his coffee." When I was asked to go back for a second and then a third interview, I was delighted that I had impressed someone that much that they thought I was worthy of meeting the CEO. When I knew it was you, all that effort went out of the window, because regardless of what you say, I can only believe that I ended up in the interview room because of you and our "friendship". That's why I'm hurt Caleb, I feel like you lied to me and I don't like liars" I hold my hand up to him as he's about to say something "I haven't finished yet" I say "I've been to the third round of interviews at another company this week and I think they might offer me the job, but I really wanted a job in your Company. That's why I'm upset because I really wanted this job and now I won't get it." I look down, because I'm really upset and I don't want to cry again.

Caleb slides his hand across the table and puts it on top of mine, I look up at him and we stare into each others eyes for a moment, then I move my hand from under his. "Tasha, the fact that you got to the third stage of interviews was on your own, I had nothing to do with it. I know you won't believe me but it's true. They are already considering you for the job, the meeting with me was supposed to seal the deal. Why can't you take the job? I don't understand, can we not be friends?"

"I can't work with you Caleb, I kissed you, how can I work with you knowing that I did that?" I shake my head as if I'm trying to work it all out.

"Tasha, I kissed you, yes you kissed me back, but I instigated it. If I promise to be good would you consider changing your mind? Please" he's trying to give me puppy dog eyes, so I laugh

"Really! You think that's going to work?" he laughs back at me "no, but it made you smile"

"I'm going to come clean with you now, I'm going to lay my feelings down on the table and I want you to listen until I'm finished, I did that for you and I want you to do the same for me" I nod because I'm too interested in what he has to say.

"OK, so when you fell into my life I had hit rock bottom where women were concerned, I had a very bad experience with a serious romance. I won't go into too much detail, but it hit me bad and I have stayed away from women since then. I couldn't believe my eyes when you were dancing, I was intrigued and fascinated at the same time, then when you fell and threw your drink at me, I knew this was an opportunity sent to me to bring you into my life. I know it all sounds soppy but it's true, I need you in my life, I need your friendship. It scares me, but I can't stop thinking about you, when I saw you being literally dragged out of Jesters, I thought that I would kill the guy, how can anyone treat you like that, you are so beautiful and deserve to be treated as if you are a rare gem. I know now you're married and I understand that we can't be together in that way, but I still want you to be my friend. I want to help you if you ever need help, I want to be there for you and I want to help you grow. I don't date married women so you're safe! But I do need you Tasha, I don't know why, I just do!" he had moved his hand over the top of mine during his speech and is rubbing it and it feels wonderful, warm, safe and it feels like home and that scares me.

"Wow Caleb, I don't know what to say. Thank you I suppose, no one has ever said anything like that to me before, it was very moving. I like our chats and want to continue with them, but I also need you to remember that I am married and intend to stay that way" I hear him mutter under his breath "mores the pity" but I ignore him.

"I know you are Tasha, believe me I know you are and I will respect that but just remember I'm here if you need anything, anything at all ok?"

He has raised his hand to cup my cheek "Please tell me the truth about what happened Tasha I need to know." I pull away from his hand, I'm mad with him, but I just can't help myself, I crave his touch!

I tell him some of what happened, but I can't tell him everything that happened, I'm just too mad with him. He needs to know what his messages do to me and what a difficult position he puts me in. "The other day you sent me a text and I read it and lied to Felix about who it was, he didn't find out, but he didn't like that I told him Kammie, that's my best friend, wanted me to go over for a girls night" I can feel myself hyperventilating just thinking about what happened "he dragged me out of the car and into the house and then, then he punched me in the face" the tears are now rolling down my cheek again, Caleb brushes a tear away. I don't tell him the rest of what happened, I just can't verbalise it to anyone yet, I don't really understand it myself.

"We had words the next morning and then I walked out after that and didn't go back for hours. I decided after I had spoken to you that I married Felix, for better or for worse and that I needed to try again, I need to do that for myself." I slowly look up into his eyes.

"Can I talk now?" he asks, I nod. He stands up and walks out of the coffee shop, I cry because I don't know if he is coming back, maybe he thinks I'm damaged goods and I'm not worthy of having him in my life. After about 2 minutes he comes back and I can see there is blood on his knuckles, I take his hand and start to clean up the blood with a napkin. "Caleb what did you do?"

"I'm sorry Tasha, the last thing you need to see is another man showing anger, I had to punch the wall, because I can't believe you've been ignoring me this week when this has happened to you. I would have been there for you, you didn't need to go through this alone you know."

"Did you tell anyone?" he asks and I shake my head.

"No Caleb, no one would believe me, they all think Felix is the perfect man"

"Well he's far from that Tasha, I can't let you go

back to that house, who knows what might happen to you."

"Caleb you can't stop me!" I say getting angry again.

"Tasha, I can't stand seeing you get hurt time and time again, it kills me to see you in pain and seeing you so unhappy" he says.

"Why Tasha?" he says and I can hear his voice shaking with emotion.

"Why did you go back? I don't understand, why?"

"Because I married him, I love him" I see Caleb flinch "I need to try again, to try and make this marriage work, I can't run out after the first "blip" in our marriage"

"Tasha this is more than a blip, he has hit you, and I'm sure he pushed you down the stairs. Did he do any of this before you got married? Why has he started now?" Caleb's eyes are darting all over the place like he has a thousand questions and needs them all answering.

"No he didn't do any of this before we got married, he was the perfect man, really attentive, bought me gifts and romanced me. I don't know what went wrong, but everytime I leave the house, he thinks I am going to leave him. He even puts my clothes out every day so that I don't show any of my body off to anyone. I don't know what to do" I put my head into my hands again, I feel really drained of emotion and I take another sip of my coffee.

"I'm sorry Tasha, I don't really understand why you haven't told anyone, why you haven't got someone to confide in to help you through this, if that's what you want."

I look at him and say "I have you now Caleb, I can

talk to you, I don't know why, but I can, you make me feel protected."

He smiles "Good, I want to protect you, all the time, but I know I can't and that kills me Tasha" he finishes his coffee.

I stand up because I feel like I need to get out of here, away from Caleb and his questions.

"Caleb I need to go back to work, I'm still angry with you but not as much as I was before" I say touching his face, I feel like I need to have one last touch to help me get through the rest of the day. I have a lot to be thinking about and I need to do that on my own."

"OK Tasha, I know why you are mad with me, I still think you should take the job when they offer it to you, I understand why you wouldn't. Let me know everything is ok later on please Tasha" I nod and we walk out of the coffee shop. He walks me back to my car and then when I'm about to climb into the car he says to me "I'm sorry Tasha, for lying to you and I'm sorry for what you are going through, but I promise I will be here for you and I won't pressurise you for anything more than friendship ok." I smile at him and then get into the car and close the door.

I feel a little bit sad that he won't be pressurising me, I kind of enjoyed it, but I also know that I can't take this any further. I pull out of my parking space and wave at him and then drive to work.

20

THE REST OF THE DAY passes with meeting after meeting and then its time to go home. Kammie had rung me during the day to find out how the interview went, I just told her that it went ok. She asks me if I'm ok as I'm very quiet, but I say I'm tired. When I get home, I change into something more comfortable and then start making dinner. When Felix comes home, dinner is waiting for him on the table, just how he likes it. It's easier just to give him what he wants to avoid any outbursts.

"Hi babe, how was your interview, I didn't get time to talk to you today?" I know he is only asking to be polite, he has already made it clear that he wants me to get the other job.

"It was ok, I'm not sure I'll be offered it though, I think the CEO is Caleb Hunt, isn't that the customer who withdrew their business when we were at the ball? I think he realised I was your wife, so I probably won't get it" I smile, but inside I'm sad.

"Really? Well you don't want to work for him

anyway, I heard he is a tyrant to work for and he always hits on the pretty girls. You definitely don't want to work there" he spits these words out. I gasp a little, maybe I misread Caleb if this is his reputation as others see him, maybe I'm not the first he has tried to seduce. It upsets me a little, but I look at Felix and smile "No maybe not, I'd have to be offered the job first anyway, I'm only speculating"

After dinner we are sat on the couch with a glass of wine each when my phone rings, my heart flip flops a little as I think it might be Caleb, but then I know he wouldn't ring me, he would text me. Felix looks at me as I rush to get my phone and answer it "Hi Tasha speaking"

"Natasha, hi this is Debbie from Clifton Associates, I hope it's not too late to ring you. We were very impressed with you on Wednesday and the CEO agreed with us, you would be perfect for the job and we would like to discuss the terms with you."

"Wow, that's great news, yes that would be good" I say smiling at Felix and trying to tell him that I was being offered the job with the Clifton Associates.

"OK well we want to speed this up so can we email the details to you and then you can look over them and ring us on Monday morning, we are really keen to get you on board sooner rather than later" she says.

"That would be great, thanks very much. I look forward to receiving your email. Thanks again and goodnight" I hang up the phone and see Felix looking at me for clarification of which job it is I'm being offered.

"It was the job with Clifton Associates, they offered me the job, they are emailing the details over to me and they want me to look over them over the weekend and contact them on Monday morning" I say in one long breath because I am excited, I know I can't take the job with Caleb, so this is the next best thing.

Felix walks over to me and pulls me in for a hug, I flinch as I always do now when he comes near me, but I sink into his hug because he is happy, and life is better when Felix is happy.

"Well done babe, I knew you would do it. I'm delighted for you. I'll go turn the computer on and then we can look over the contract together. You go open another bottle of wine and we can celebrate" he stands and walks towards the office.

"Felix can we go out and celebrate tomorrow with Kammie and maybe Luca, it would be fun" I smile, we always had fun when we went out with the gang.

"No, I don't want to share you Tasha, if we go out we go out alone, not with anyone else, OK" he nearly shouts the last word and I know I need to back down. I don't know when I will see my friend again, but I won't be defeated though.

I walk into the kitchen to get another bottle of wine and I text Kammie to tell her I've been offered the job at the Facilities Management Company, she is delighted and wants to know when we are going out to celebrate. Great minds think alike.

"Felix wants to celebrate together if you know what I mean"

"Yeah I do, but tell him that he can't monopolise you, we want to celebrate with you too!"

"We can go for lunch on Tuesday if you want, I can

make sure that I have a long business lunch organised"

"Sounds good to me, but don't bring the car, there might be some alcohol involved"

"Definitely sounds like a plan to me. See you in Piccolinos at 1.00pm on Tuesday yeah?"

"See you then bitch"

I laugh to myself, I don't know how Felix will take my long liquid lunch, but for once I don't care. Kammie is excited for me and she's my best friend, he really can't stop me seeing her. While I have the phone out I send a quick text off to Caleb.

"Hi I'm good, but just wanted you to know that the other company offered me a job this evening and they are sending the contract over for me to look at this weekend and I'm to go back to them on Monday morning"

"I know I should congratulate you, but I really wanted you to work for me Tasha, but if it's what you want then congratulations. Keep in touch this weekend please"

He's so demanding but in a nice way I suppose.

"Yes boss! LOL, I'm off to have some wine to celebrate, have a good weekend Caleb"

"Thanks, it would be better if we could go out and celebrate your news, but I know that won't happen x"

I really have mixed feelings about Caleb, he just confuses me so much. I turn and Felix is coming into the kitchen with my contract, I quickly delete my messages from Kammie and Caleb and put my phone in my pocket. We sit at the breakfast bar with the contract, a pen and a glass of wine.

After about half an hour, my phone rings again, this time it is Helen from Blue Eye, I know what's coming next!

"Hi Tasha speaking" I say.

"Hi it's Helen here from Blue Eye, I hear your meeting with Mr Hunt went well today, congratulations, we wanted to offer you the position here with us, but we just needed his approval, which he gave us this evening.Can we email the contract and terms for the position over to you for your perusal?" she asks.

"Erm yeah I suppose, sorry I'm a bit flabbergasted, yes, yes of course you can, thanks, talk to you soon"

I come off the phone and just look at Felix with my mouth open.

"Tasha what is it?" He asks.

"That was Helen from Blue Eye, they offered me the Administration Manager's job and they're emailing the contract to me to check over" I say and reach for my glass and take a big gulp of wine.

"Wow Tasha being offered two jobs in one evening, that's some achievement. You must have really impressed Mr Hunt. What did you say to him? Did you insinuate you'd sleep with him?" He's in my face now. How did this lovely evening go pear shaped in just a few minutes?

"Felix don't start on me, I didn't insinuate anything and why did you not say that about the first company. Is that because you know the Operations Manager and didn't tell me. Did you make a deal with him or something?" I'm getting really mad. He's once again spoiling some good news that I've been given.

"Felix please just sit down, calm down and let's go through the contracts and see which one is better. We can do a positive/negative list if you want, please just be happy for me" I'm surprised when he backs down, I really didn't expect him to, that means he really is trying.

"Sorry babe, I just got jealous because I know Caleb Hunt is a player that's all" he sits back down and we spend the next two hours going over both contracts and finishing off the bottle of wine.

"Felix, I have to go to bed I'm exhausted I hope you don't mind" I kiss him on the head.

"No problem babe I'll tidy up and lock up then I'll come up too" he kisses me on the lips. I only allow him to put a kiss on my lips, I don't let him put his tongue in my mouth, I'm not ready for that yet!

When I get upstairs I send a quick text to Caleb.

"Oh you are playing so dirty. I can't believe you did that! That is so not fair!"

"What are you talking about ?????"

"You know damn well what I mean, Mr Not So Innocent!!"

"I couldn't let you think that we weren't going to offer you the job, you deserve the job and that is nothing to do with me or what I think of you! You needed to be thinking about my position too"

"Well now I have to consider the two jobs although Felix doesn't want me to take your job because you are a player and you might try to bed me ha ha"

"Oh I didn't think of that what a great idea ha ha.

Seriously though, you deserve the job and it should be given consideration. What are you doing now?"

"I'm getting ready for bed, I'm exhausted it's been a very emotional day"

"What do you wear in bed?"

"Caleb, please! Don't!"

"Sorry you can't knock a guy for trying. Hope you sleep well Tasha"

"Night Caleb hope you don't dream about me lol"

"Of course I will"

I don't think he can just be a friend, but knowing that he knows he can't have me, surely a little banter won't hurt. Will it??

I get into bed and take a sleeping tablet. I know I need to stop taking them but today has been emotionally draining. I very quickly fall asleep. I have an amazingly erotic dream which feels so real.

When I climax in my dream, I wake up and see Felix above me sweating and fully sated "Baby that was amazing you were so horny, I couldn't resist. I stayed downstairs for an hour or so and when I came upstairs you were moaning in your sleep and you were masturbating. I watched you for a while but then I had to join in I couldn't keep my hands off you" he leans down and kisses me on the lips. Now I realise they were his lips I felt not Caleb's! It was all a dream!

"Felix get off me, you have to stop taking advantage of me when I'm sleeping for gods sake it's not right" I'm angry now, but mainly because I realise I wanted Caleb's hands to be caressing me and not Felix's.

All of a sudden he pulls out of me and rolls onto his side and then he's right in my face "You still don't get it do you Tasha? You're my wife and I'll have you anyway, anywhere with no questions asked. Get used to it babe!" He moves away and goes into the bathroom to clean up.

Great now he's pissed at me again, what next? Will I ever get a break from Mr Aggressive. With that thought the bathroom door gets flung open and Felix looks really angry, obviously he didn't go into the bathroom to calm down. His cock is big and hard again and he storms over to me, he grabs me by the hair and drags me off the bed

"Kneel in front of me Tasha, NOW!" He's shouting so I do what he says, my head is hurting and I can see a clump of my hair in his hands. I keep repeating in my head. I will not cry. I will not cry.

He pushes me backwards so that I have my back to the bed and he grabs my hair at the nape of my neck and pulls hard to make me open my mouth. With that he pounds his cock into my mouth. All I want to do is bite down on it, but I know that would be a bad thing to do. I take him as far as I can and I look at him with pleading eyes.

"Take it all bitch, do you really think I thought you were dreaming about me. I know you were dreaming about someone else, tell me who it is bitch?" How he expects me to talk I don't know. He is pounding in and out of my mouth so hard it hurts the back of my throat.

"I want to be the one you think of when you're masturbating. Only me. Think of this moment when I'm fucking your mouth, that's what will happen again if I catch you masturbating on your own do you hear me?"

I nod my head and I try to say "Felix stop" but it just comes out all garbled.

"Oh babe that's amazing try and talk again that

really turns me on"

I try to just say something and hopefully it will make him cum and then he might stop.

"Babe you are so beautiful right now with your mouth around my cock taking me all the way. I'm going to cum and you're going to swallow it all and then you're not going to say another word to me tonight. At all. Ok?"

I nod my head. That turns him on so I'm hoping this will be over soon. He throws back his head and pushes my head against the bed and sticks his cock as far down my throat as he can and then he cums. I start to panic because I can't breathe and I feel like I'm choking.I reach out and start hitting him in the legs, he just groans so I pinch him, he groans again. I start to feel dizzy and start to pass out. Everything goes black and then I feel light, a sense of floating. I welcome this feeling, maybe this is the end. Maybe this is where all the hurt stops.

Epilogue

WHO THE HELL IS ringing me at this time of night? For gods sake it's 1o'clock, I pick the phone up and answer gruffly "yeah?"

"Luca, Luca it's me"

"What do you want Felix? It's the middle of the night" I know I sound angry and dammit I am angry.

"I'm sorry, I'm sorry Luca, I need you, I need you to come over and bring Kammie with you." Felix says, he's crying "Please before something really bad happens."

He's panicking and crying, what has he done this time? I swear to god if he's hurt Tasha again I'm going to personally kill him.

"Felix, what did you do? Tell me she's ok!" I'm getting angrier by the minute. I start getting dressed, I know he's going to need me to go to the house. He doesn't answer me, this is going to be bad I just know it!

"Felix, Felix talk to me NOW!" I'm shouting, I need him to talk to me.

"Luca, I've done it, I think I've killed her" he's

sobbing. "What will I do? I want her, I need her, Luca, I need you mate."

This sounds bad, what the hell has gone on. "Felix I'm coming, I'm just leaving my house, I'll be there in 5 minutes, quicker if I can, stay on the phone and keep talking to me ok" I know I'm pleading but he sounds like he's slipping away from me.

"Felix, FELIX, what did you do?" I'm shouting.

"I think I killed her" he sobs.

"What did you do and why do you sound strange Felix?"

"I need help Luca, I can't be without her!"

Coming 10th May 2014

"In Sickness and In Health"

The second book in the

"Til Death Us Do Part Series.

Acknowledgements

I would like to thank so many people for helping me with this series of books. Most of you don't even know how you have helped me.

Little Cozy Pace Coffee Shop for letting me sit and type my book all the time, feeding me with coffee and cakes. It became my retreat, but especially Jenny for telling me that I should go for it and write my own book. I don't think she really thought I was going to do it, but I did! Thanks Jenny x

So many people have helped me on my journey, but I want to particularly thank my official beta readers: Meg, Natasha, Claire, Nicola, Jodie and Tara, without you to steer me in the right direction, I surely would have veered off along the way. You kept me motivated and helped me to make this story the best I could. Thanks to you all xx

I also had a large amount of unofficial beta readers: my friends and family, thank you so much for your constructive criticism – it helped me with a lot of sticky points. Xx

I have to say a big thank you to the girls that I work with, you have heard me talking about "my book" and my "author friends" and "my friends in America and

Canada" and I am sure that you are sick of hearing it. Thank you for listening or pretending to listen. I love you allxx

Author L Chapman has helped me with some of the obscure things to do with writing a book and for that I will be forever grateful. Thanks Louise x

Omie, my lovely Omie, what can I say? You have given me the inspiration to just go out and write! I love your work and I love you!

My husband Alan, for putting up with the third person in our marriage – my laptop or Ipad. He hasn't seen me without either of these since last November. My children for putting up with Mummy having to type on the laptop all the time and my Mum for giving me the confidence to believe that I can do this – you always push me just the right amount and you must be fed up whenever I try something new. You knew how much this meant to me and you gave me the confidence and determination to keep going. I love you all xx

Lastly and by no means least are two very special ladies in my life. I met them through another author and they agreed to be my beta readers, but they became more than that, they became personal friends. We talk every single day, we laugh together and they give me the motivation to believe in myself. I hope some day soon that I will get to meet these lovely ladies and I know that we will have a long friendship even after my books are all written. Meg and Natasha I love you guys so much and I can't thank you enough for picking me up when I was down. xx

About the Author

I am a mother to two young children, who in turn keep me young. I live in Dublin, Ireland but, I'm originally from South Devon in the UK. I work full time in a pharmacy and write in all my spare time: in my lunch hour, when watching TV at night and anywhere the urge takes me.

I have always been interested in reading from a young age and then 2 years ago I was given a kindle as a present and it was the best thing that happened to me. I was able to read lots of books ever weeky and then I started to write reviews for all the books I read.

I took this one step further and started my own facebook page – Sparkling Pink Bookshelf. I intended to upload all of my reviews for the books I read. This was purely for pleasure and then I answered a post on facebook for someone to read for reviews and thought I had died and gone to heaven. I was reading about 7/8 books a week, the kindle made this achievable. I would read at any opportunity I could, even staying up til the small hours to finish a book. I loved it.

Then one day I was asked to beta read a book – I loved this side of it, it was so exciting. I have worked with a number of indie authors and have remained loyal to a few select authors and I beta read all their books.

After a year or more of doing this, I thought maybe I could write some of the stories that were in my head and I just decided to write and see what happened. I wrote about 70% of a story and then saw a post for the NaNoWriMo competition – to write 50,000 words in 30 days, I decided that this was a challenge I wanted to take and the Til Death Us Do Part series was born.

I am always thinking of situations that can be turned into a story and have started a few stories, which in turn will be completed and released to my readers.

I love to hear what my readers have to say about my work and please find my links below:

Goodreads:
https://www.goodreads.com/book/show/21421331-for-better-or-for-worse

Facebook:
https://www.facebook.com/authorkrissy.vas

Thank you for your support and I hope you enjoy this series of books as much as I enjoyed writing them.

Krissy V

11190093R00109

Printed in Great Britain
by Amazon.co.uk, Ltd.,
Marston Gate.